Steve Barber is a confident introvert who has greatly enjoyed writing since his early 20s. He has had a long, diverse and satisfying career in the health and beauty industry, and in addition to *German Girls*, he has written many children's stories and poems for his beloved Sarah and Dan. Steve lives with his wonderful wife, Ine, and two cats on the south coast of England. His favourite authors are Anne Tyler, Chris Stewart and Alexander McCall Smith. Steve enjoys walking, wildlife watching and being by the sea.

Steve Barber

GERMAN GIRLS

AUSTIN MACAULEY PUBLISHERS™

LONDON • CAMBRIDGE • NEW YORK • SHARJAH

A CIP catalogue record for this title is available from the British Library.

ISBN 9781528972949 (Paperback)
ISBN 9781528997362 (ePub e-book)

www.austinmacauley.com

First Published 2023
Austin Macauley Publishers Ltd®
1 Canada Square
Canary Wharf
London
E14 5AA

Part 1
August 1978
Swanage, Dorset

Saturday

We were stuck. Stationary cars as far as the eye could see in front of us and then around a corner. We had set off half an hour before our parents to be sure that we would all arrive at much the same time at 'The Lymes' hotel in Swanage. Mum and Dad had stayed there before and promised us that it was a comfortable hotel right on the seafront with fantastic food. I had chosen to drive us both down to the coast in my old mini clubman despite its regular habit of overheating in traffic jams.

That, at least, would give us the opportunity to go off on our own from time to time or come home early if it got really unbearable.

It had seemed a pretty poor option at the time, a family holiday on the south coast in Swanage or no summer holiday at all. I had left college in 1976 after passing my 'A' levels and had been working for eighteen months, I was saving to move away from home. Having not gone to university, I was keen to establish some independence for myself and experience some of what a lot of 19-year-olds already had, even if it was likely to be only a rented room and some space of my own.

Starting work at seventeen with good 'A' levels still meant low pay and a slog to catch up with the high-flying graduates that big multinationals really sought after in the late 1970s. I could have gone to uni had I had an inkling about what I wanted to study…but I hadn't. Not well rounded enough in science to go for anything really technical…Physics and chemistry required too much maths for my liking…not interested in accountancy or becoming a doctor or dentist, so I had opted to apply to large multinationals to get in as a management trainee and had been offered places by more than one. Encouraged by this and the limitless opportunities they boasted about in marketing, purchasing or logistics, I had accepted the highest offer and spent twelve months moving from one central department to another gaining experience of how the company worked and in which markets it sold its vast array of consumer goods. I had been promoted out of my management trainee position into a permanent role and was one of only three left from the original trainee intake of fifteen.

Living at home wasn't bad either, with loving parents, a sister who was excellent company, and the low rent for high quality accommodation and wonderful home cooking made it possible for me to put a significant amount of my salary each month towards some independence.

So, Swanage it had to be. At least, it would be a week off work. My younger sister, Sam, was coming along too so that would make it much more bearable. I was a bit nervous about the mini overheating, as it was a scorching hot morning, but had been reliably told by a friend that the best way to reduce the problem when stuck in traffic was to roll the windows down, put the heater on maximum and turn the fan on full blast. "Sucks the heat away from the engine," he assured me. I had hoped it wouldn't come to that but felt a little comforted that I had something I could try if we hit a problem…which we had at Wareham, where a dual carriage way became a single lane and there were roadworks and temporary traffic lights that weren't working properly. We sat for twenty-five minutes moving no more than fifty yards. It was stiflingly hot in the car with the sun shining directly on us, the heater full on and the fan blasting hot air past our feet and faces and out of the open windows. The engine temperature indicator needle hovered ominously just below the red danger line but didn't venture over it. We sat in silence, trying to pretend that we were listening to the music playing on my portable ~~Philips~~ cassette player sat on the back seat but were both willing that little black needle to move no higher.

At last, we were through the temporary traffic lights and moving at a good speed again. The engine temperature needle had returned to its /normal\ zone and we relaxed, laughing and joking about the coming week.

"So you reckon you're going to pull this week, do you, Sam?" I teased.

"Oh yeah." She ~~giggled~~ laughed. "There are bound to be some dishy foreign waiters in the hotel."

"What? In Swanage?" ~~I laughed~~. "More likely to be OAPs who can't deliver more than half a bowl of soup without spilling it!" really? not that funny

We both laughed ~~uncontrollably~~ until the car in front broke unexpectedly and I had to do an emergency stop so as not to hit it. After a moment's silence, we both fell about laughing again. Neither of us was ~~very~~ lucky with romance so we had found a safe mutual ground where we joked about it.

9

We arrived in Swanage twenty minutes later and quickly found ‘The Lymes’ hotel. It was a medium-sized, two-storey, white-washed building. ~~Looked 1950s' style to me.~~ To the left was a large car park with plenty of empty spaces to park in. Our parent's car wasn't there so we got out and had a walk around.

"Looks popular!" joked Sam, casting her eyes around the half full car park.

"~~All the more~~ Lots of Spanish waiters for you!" I teased.

We walked past the entrance to the reception into a ~~good-sized~~ garden with sun-loungers, garden chairs and tables with big, cream outdoor parasols ~~printed in dark green with the words 'The Lymes' all around.~~ The grass ~~was~~ closely mown and well edged.

"~~Very nice,~~" I said, "but where is everybody?"

"It's lunchtime," said Sam, "so I suppose they're all enjoying the fabulous food Mum promised."

She was right. We walked around the paved edge of the garden and saw ~~that~~ the large circular restaurant was reasonably full of guests. The tables were set around the edge of a huge semi-circular bay window extension overlooking the garden. We ~~continued our walk to~~ the cliff-edge of the garden and ~~stood looking~~ out to sea. To our right was the main part of Swanage town with its seafront and promenade, with the usual English seaside attractions including a small funfair at the far end. From the hotel garden, there were steep steps down to the shingle and sand beach which was 'For Private Use of the Guests at The Lymes Hotel' according to a sign at the top. After ten minutes or so, I said, "Well, it certainly looks very nice."

"Hmm," said Sam, "let's go and see if they've arrived yet."

We walked back through the garden and out to the car park. Our parents had just got out of their car and were stretching their legs and looking approvingly around.

"Well done, Paul," said Dad, "you beat us!"

"Not intentionally," I replied truthfully. "We got held up for ages at Wareham."

"So did we," said Dad, clearly annoyed about it. "Some fool had overheated, broken down and stopped right in the middle of the road. We had to wait whilst someone gave them a push into the nearest pub car park."

Sam and I exchanged glances knowing that was nearly us!

"Let's go and get checked in," said Mum, quick to get things back onto the positive.

"Good idea, darling," Dad responded. "We may be in time for some lunch."

We hauled the cases from the back of Dad's large estate car and lumbered them into the bright reception area. In front of us were two classy polished wooden desks, back-to-back with two smartly uniformed young women manning them. To the right was a low, round glass-topped coffee table with four comfortable-looking, high-backed wicker chairs with deep cushions. The sun had forced its way through the open venetian blinds in strong horizontal bands which gleamed and reflected off the top of the table surface onto the white ceiling making it look as if a modern impressionist painter had been hired to do the interior decoration.

Mum and Sam sat down whilst Dad and I checked in, gave our car registration numbers and chose from the rooms that were still available. Sam and I were sharing, which was a bit odd for a brother and sister of 19 and 16, but no one commented. Dad opted for the larger, more luxurious room offered at the front of the hotel. In contrast, I chose the smaller of the other two available rooms because it was at the back of the hotel with a window overlooking the garden and the sea. Both Sam and I loved to hear the sound of the sea at night so I knew she would approve.

"Just dump your bags in your room and meet us in the restaurant in five minutes," Dad directed as he carted their huge cases off towards the lift. Mum gave us a giggling 'over-the-shoulder' glance and followed him.

Sam and I carried our much smaller luggage past reception, past the lift and down a corridor with various framed colour photos of the proprietors with happy-looking guests in the garden. There was one of the head chef and his team lined up like a victorious football squad and then some views to the left and right of the hotel from dawn, through midday and dusk and finally into the night. We turned left then sharply right towards the back of the hotel. Our room was number 8 and was in the far right-hand corner at the back of the hotel. There was a shower room, a wardrobe and two single beds separated by just enough room for a medium-sized person to squeeze between. In its favour was the fact that it was double aspect with one of the windows opening onto the garden and the seafront.

We dumped our cases on the beds and opened the windows. We stood in silence and listened. The sound of the sea slowly 'breathing' in and out drifted into the room. In, as little waves drew small pebbles and shells up the beach. Out, as it pushed them back across the wet sand. We listened for a minute or two and then remembered Dad's insistence that we join them in the restaurant straight away. I locked the room and we walked back along the corridor, past the lift and into the restaurant. We could hear the clanging and chatter from the adjacent kitchen. The restaurant door was open so I led the way in but had to stop abruptly as two giggling girls were hurrying out, looking back over their shoulders into the restaurant rather than where they were going. We avoided collision, but only just. The older of the two turned at the last second and saw me. She stopped, her younger sister bumping into her from behind and opened her deep blue eyes wide with surprise.

"Aahh, ooh, Zorry!" she blurted in a strong German accent. I stepped aside, smiling and they hurried out, just about suppressing wild giggles...which grew to uncontrollable laughter as they ran past reception towards the lift. I looked after them as they went. Both had blonde hair and good, deep tans. The older girl had thick, curly, yellow-blonde hair cut just above her shoulder height.

The younger one had lighter blonde, long, straight hair half-way down her back. They were about Sam's height, say around five foot six.

"Come on," said Sam in a mock stern voice. "Lunch, remember?" And she walked past me into the restaurant. I looked after her, still a bit stunned and followed, saying nothing.

Mum and Dad had already found an empty table by the window on the far side of the restaurant, and were heavily involved in trying to decide what to order from the large menus in their hands. Sat at a table next to them were a couple, similar to them in age, sipping coffee. From my limited language studies at school, these people looked German to

13

me, I remembered pictures from German textbooks and was sure I was right. Languages came quite easily to me so I had enjoyed their study and paid particular attention to a lot of detail. We walked around the edge of a small rectangular dance floor towards our table, and as we reached it, the German-looking gentleman said, "Zorry bowt zat. Zey vill go svimming!"

I smiled. "That's okay…er…*kein* problem. *Danke*!"

"*Bitte*," he replied politely, smiling in appreciation at my using his native language.

"Bloody show-off," hissed Sam under her breath, prodding me in the back.

We sat down at the table with Mum and Dad and waited until they had made their choices.

"They've changed the menu since we were here last time," said Dad, "but it still looks excellent." Sam chose a salad, poor girl was always on a diet, and I joined her, suddenly not feeling as hungry as I had an hour earlier.

"How about a walk along the clifftop after we've had our lunch and unpacked?" offered Dad.

"Oh, I thought I might go for a swim," I replied. "It may not be as sunny tomorrow." I got another mock glare from Sam, but she agreed that we shouldn't waste the opportunity whilst the sun shone.

We ate our lunch, chatting about the drive down, the good points about the hotel and compiled a list of things to do if the weather turned less summery.

"Corfe Castle is quite interesting," said Mum. "We enjoyed our visit last time, didn't we, dear?"

"Yes," replied Dad. "It's only a short drive, and although it's just ruins now, you can make out the basic architecture, and there are some stunning views across the Dorset heathlands. You'll be able to get some good photos, Paul."

I had bought a 35mm TLL, German 'Practica' camera not too long ago and enjoyed trying to be creative with it. My mum and sisters were very artistic and drew and painted well. This was my only way of competing with them!

Lunch was as good as it had promised to be and we were soon back in our room unpacking. We had arranged to go down to the beach at our leisure and meet Mum and Dad there. I finished my unpacking quickly and stood around waiting for Sam, looking out of our window.

"In a hurry, are we?" Sam teased.

"All right, all right," I conceded, "but you have to admit she is rather lovely."

"Very pretty," agreed Sam and after a pause said, "but perhaps a bit young."

"No!" I objected. "She's definitely seventeen!"

Sam giggled and continued unpacking slowly.

"I'll go and find us a good spot on the beach," I said impatiently. "I'll pop back to the car and get the ball and beach stuff. See you down there."

Sam was still smirking and shaking her head as I left the room.

In the car park, I noticed the German gentleman walking off towards a public footpath that I guessed led along the clifftop. He was slim and slightly bent forward in stature, about five foot eight with a head that seemed just a bit too big for his body. His hair was wispy, dark brown and he wore round, steel-framed, silver glasses. He had the look of a scientist of some kind, I guessed he was about the same age as Dad. He was carrying some serious photographic equipment, ~~tripod, long zoom lens and so on~~. Might prove a good subject for conversation later on I thought. I got the ball and some beach rugs from the boot, ~~locked the car~~ and made my way across the hotel garden and down the steps to the beach.

It was still quite breezy, but most of the guests had decided to at least try some time in the sun on the beach. Very few were actually in the sea and closer to I had to admit that it looked colder than w~~hen looking down from the clifft~~op. Still, this was no time to be chickening out. I looked around for the German girls and saw them sat with their mother with towels wrapped around their shoulders, ~~whilst~~ their mother ~~was still~~ in her dress with a cardigan on reading a book. ~~I had noted earlier how similar~~ She was in height, shape and facial appearance to my mum. ~~She had~~ an elegance about her. Her hair was light brown and wavy, carefully looked after and well cut. Her face was /open\ and attractive, with smiling eyes. She has a sense of strong calmness about her.

I put the beach things down about ten yards from them and got ready to go for a swim. The top part of the beach was all shingle and I tried to put on a brave face as I strode across it towards the sea, sharp pebbles jutting painfully into ~~the soft parts of~~ my insteps. I gratefully reached the softer sand and waded ~~purposefully~~ into the small waves. The water was freezing, but I kept going until the water was half-way up my thighs then I had to hold my breath and dive forward before common sense ~~got the better of me~~. As always, once the initial shock was over ~~and the water had covered head and shoulders,~~ it didn't seem so bad. I swam ~~front crawl~~ for a while and then turned over onto my ~~back~~ hoping that the sun would warm me up a bit,…it didn't. Then I swam ~~breaststrok~~e parallel with the

16

beach to see if Sam had arrived yet...but she hadn't. I turned and swam away from the hotel back towards where the ~~German~~ girls were sitting. They had piled up some pebbles and were throwing other pebbles at the tower to try and knock it down. The older girl looked up a couple of times but neither made a move to join me ~~in the sea~~. I wondered how long I could keep this up and turned and swam a bit further out then back towards the hotel. Thankfully, Sam was coming down the steps, which gave me the excuse to swim back and wade out calling to her so that she could see where my beach things were. She dumped her bag and towel on the rug.

"Come on!" I called "It's not too cold. Bring the ball, ~~too please~~."

Sam looked doubtful but ~~gamefully~~ made her way across the shingle and onto the sand. As the first small waves lapped over her ankle, she shrieked.

"~~Good grief~~, you must be mad!"

"Once you're in and swimming, it's fine," I lied. "The sun keeps the top part of the water warmer."

Sam ~~hurled~~ the ball at me ~~and splashe~~d water up her arms to try and get used to the temperature. ~~She~~ waded out another few feet.

"You'd better be right," she warned, let out another ~~banshee~~ shriek and half ran, half dived ~~into the surf~~. Amazingly, she agreed with me. Sam never felt the cold the way I did. We tried to keep warm by putting as much effort as possible into our game of catch, running waist deep in the water and diving to catch the ball.

The ~~German girls~~ had grown bored of their pebble throwing game and the younger one had stood up and was clearly trying to persuade her sister to try the sea. Eventually, she gingerly discarded her towel and they hobbled across the shingle together holding hands for support and laughing and shrieking. They reached the water's edge and waded in knee-deep. I watched as they both opened their eyes wide and sucked in deep breaths at the shock of the cold. They were talking quickly in German, half shivering, half laughing, and I couldn't make out a word. I sensed that they were about to turn around and head back up the beach so I threw the ball high towards them and the younger one shouted, "Come on!!!"

She reached up instinctively and jumped to catch the ball. She caught it athletically but then stumbled backwards on her heels, dropped the ball, wobbled with her arms and hands stretched out behind her and sat down in the surf, the small waves splashing her neck. The older girl doubled up with laughter at the sight of her sister sat like that in the cold sea. That was it! The younger girl hauled herself up and started to chase her sister, running and shooting water at her with both hands. The older girl screamed and started to run away back towards the sandy beach, but the water slowed her down and her sister blocked her escape. Sam and I were both laughing now and the whole beach was watching the noisy drama. With strong strides forward, the younger girl forced her sister deeper and deeper into the sea despite her mock pleadings and they both ended up diving headlong into the waves.

We spent a chilly twenty minutes throwing the ball to each other and chasing around to keep warm. Then we all waded back up the beach. The cold had prevented us from having any sort of proper introductions, but once we were drier and warmer, we swapped names and shook hands, as is the tradition in Germany. They were seventeen and fifteen, Heidi and Julia Wortmann and they lived with their parents in Frankfurt. Their father was a university professor in biology, ~~specialising in botany.~~ They both spoke excellent English ~~with Heidi, understandably, being more advance~~d. They had already been at 'The Lymes' for a week, and were staying another fortnight. Heidi said that the first week had been ~~very~~ boring because the weather was bad and there were no interesting people at the hotel. I explained that I spoke a little German and they seemed reasonably impressed when we had a short conversation in their native language. *irrelevant detail*

We were now drier and warmer, ~~and had been properly introduced~~ so we built another tower of pebbles and started to destroy it. Mum and Dad arrived and paddled in the cold sea holding hands. We got bored, Discarded our towels, and hobbled onto the sandy part of the beach for a game of catch. The breeze had died down a bit, enough for me to show off by spinning the ball on one finger 'Harlem Globetrotter' style, and we threw the ball to one another with increasing speed, laughing when one of us dropped the ball or did a poor throw. Wearing only her bikini, I was easily able to see that Heidi had a great figure as well as a ~~good, deep~~ tan, pretty face and lovely hair. *poorly expressed   you said this before*

My parents and Mrs Wortmann soon agreed that it was too cold for them and that they would prefer to be sheltered from the breeze in the hotel garden and so made their way back up the steep steps. The four of us stayed on the beach for another thirty minutes, until around four o'clock and then conceded that it would be nicer in the warmer garden. We joined our parents, ordered cups of tea and made polite conversation. Mrs Wortmann and her daughters filled us in with the diary of events at 'The Lymes'. There were dance evenings and games evenings…bingo and some other board games and so on. The garden was now much fuller than it had been earlier, more guests must have arrived, unpacked and started to relax.

At five o'clock, a smiling Mr Wortmann joined us. He carefully set all his elaborate photographic equipment on the ground and told us that he had a great afternoon. "Making fotos of zer Bog Asphodel and Dorset Heass. Zis heasslant ve have not in Germany," he said, "not *in zer nahe* of Frankfurt!" (I knew that '*in zer nahe*' meant 'in the region of' or 'near to') He had also seen a sand lizard and a 'silver studded blue' butterfly and was clearly thrilled. I told him, in my best German, that he should go for a swim in the sea as the water was wonderfully warm. His daughters giggled loudly, but his wife warned him that she did not want to see him with blue toes! More cheerful conversation, laughter and intermittent tea drinking followed until it was around six o'clock. Both families were ready for showers and a rest before dinner, so we shook hands, parted company and went back to our respective rooms.

"Well, I hope there are some good-looking waiters for me tonight!" said Sam jokingly when we were back inside Room 8. "You seem to have got your chance already and we haven't been here more than an afternoon!"

"Don't worry, Sam," I said half seriously, "there will probably be some handsome bastard staying here this week and I won't get a look in!"

"Don't you worry!" Sam laughed. "If there is, he's mine and Heidi will have to be content with you!"

We showered, lazed around and read books, me frantically trying to remember as much German as I could.

It's funny how sometimes when you're in a quiet environment with someone or some people that you know very well and are all concentrating on the same thing, exams or just reading…there seems to be a synergistic energy/effect that helps everybody. I felt that as I read my book knowing that Sam was deep in her book too, not thinking about anything else, just enjoying concentrating on what she was reading, forming images in her mind. The time flew by and we suddenly realised we needed to get dressed and go down for dinner. We'd arranged to meet Mum and Dad in the restaurant at seven thirty. When we arrived, the restaurant was already pretty full, and we had to take one of the few tables that was left. The Wortmann family was already seated at a table on the other side of the room, so no chance this evening to make much further contact. I had a good look around at the other guests, hoping not to find a stunningly handsome rival and, to my relief, found none. There were a lot of families with pre-teenage children and several families much our age. One with two very plain daughters with pale skin and straight, dark hair, cut in appallingly bad 'bobs'.

Another with one son who was a bit on the tubby side with blonde hair and a fat, red face. I was especially pleased to note that he had no dress sense! I prided myself with a good sense of style when it came to clothes and spent a good amount of my available cash on them.

As the restaurant was so busy, we waited patiently for a waiter to come and take our orders. Eventually, a short, wiry waiter with slicked back dark hair and a pale, slightly withery complexion arrived at our table with his order pad. He spoke with a strong Scottish accent and introduced himself as Alec. We ordered our meals and spent the evening enjoying some wonderful food and planning the next day's activities. Sunday evening, the Wortmanns had told us was a 'Dance Evening', and although they hadn't said what kind of music was played, it seemed obvious to me that this would be a great opportunity to get to know Heidi a lot better. We planned a walk along the clifftops to 'Old Harry Rocks' and then an afternoon on the beach if the weather was as the forecast had promised. What with the drive, the cold sea, plenty of 'ozone' and a good amount of food and wine inside us by ten thirty we were pretty tired and so went to bed. I lay with the window ajar listening to the soothing sound of the sea and wondering if this was going to be a very much better holiday than I had imagined.

"Sam," I whispered, not wanting to wake her if she was asleep, "this place is good, isn't it?"

"Hmmm?" she grunted, half asleep. "Oh yes, it's good." And then nothing, her breathing taking on that rhythm of someone who has just fallen peacefully asleep.

Sunday

I expected to dream wonderful, romantic dreams but in fact woke up at six thirty having not dreamt at all. Gulls were screeching and the sun was already bright through the window (we both slept with the curtains only three quarters drawn, something our mum had always done and somehow we'd followed). I sat up slowly in bed and looked through the gap in the curtains. There was a light breeze blowing making the garden parasols spin gently around, their green fringes waving. A flock of starlings were chasing madly from one part of the lawn to another, their heads pumping back and forth like clockwork toys, but no sign of any other life. I lay back down relaxing with that feeling of being on holiday and not having to rush to do anything. The light breeze was quite cool and had kept our room at a nice temperature…just cool enough for a good, long sleep and for it still to be warm enough under the sheets. Sam's breathing was still the steady in and out of a human being not yet awake so I closed my eyes and drifted into the kind of half-sleep that leaves you woolly headed and slightly disorientated when you re-awake, which I did at just before eight o'clock. I got up, shaved, brushed my teeth and, seeing that she still hadn't woken up, gave Sam a gentle nudge.

"Wake up, Sam, it's eight fifteen," I hissed. "Breakfast at nine, remember?"

"Hmm?" she groaned. Half turning over and making as if to go back to sleep.

"Sam!" I said, at normal volume. "Time to wake up! You've had nine hours' sleep and we should be at breakfast soon."

She opened her eyes slowly, made eye contact, nodded and said, "I'll get up in five minutes."

How is it that women can get ready in half the time it takes men? Anyway, I went out for a walk around the garden to give Sam the privacy she needed to get ready. There was no one else out there, but I could hear the clanking and muddled jumble of many conversations from the restaurant where, judging from the mouth-watering smells that were drifting across the garden, kippers, eggs and bacon, toast and marmalade were being consumed in vast quantities accompanied by (maybe Kenyan?) coffee. I walked to the top of the steps that led down to the beach. There was a group of six or seven black-headed gulls standing very still about twenty yards to the left of the last step. They didn't move their heads nor wings nor legs. I wondered if this was some kind of gull beach game…who can stay rigidly still the longest! When another two gulls flew in low and joined them causing them all to take off, fly in a wide circle and then land again ten yards further up the beach, adopting the same statue-like positions. I was totally absorbed by the show and didn't sense someone coming up behind me.

"Gut morning. Are you going to svim in zer varm sea?"

I jumped, span around and looked into the smiling face of Herr Wortmann. He was grinning from ear to ear, delighted to have startled me and pleased with his joke. Having recovered, I laughed with him.

"*Noch nicht, aber veilleicht spatter, nach Mittag,*" I replied (not now, but maybe be later this afternoon). This was a big mistake because he launched into a long and complicated paragraph in German, the content of which I could not really understand, just barely picked out a few words. I apologised in German and asked him to repeat more slowly.

He replied in excellent English. He and his family were going to look around Bournemouth today to see the town without too many shoppers in the way. After lunch, they intended to go to the beach. Brilliant! I thought, perhaps the sea may have warmed up a bit today. We made our way back towards the restaurant making simple, polite conversation in German. The rest of the Wortmann family were waiting in the small reception area. I greeted Mrs Wortmann, Julia and Heidi, allowing my eye contact to linger and intensify. She was certainly not shy and held my eyes with hers, smiling openly. It was 8.55 and the Wortmanns went into breakfast whilst I waited for Sam and our parents. Predictably, Dad arrived first, Mum and Sam followed. Whilst we enjoyed our meals, we checked our Ordinance Survey map for the best route to 'Old Harry Rocks'. It would probably take two and a half hours to get there and back, allowing time for a sit down and a good look once we got there.

"Have you got your camera ready, Paul?" asked Dad.

"Not yet, but it will only take a minute," I replied.

We finished our breakfasts, went back to our rooms and got ready for our walk.

"This is going to be spectacular," I told Sam. "The chalk clifftops just keep going and going until they reach 'Old Harry Rocks' where the headland turns ninety degrees and sea erosion has left two or maybe three huge parts of the cliff isolated in the water similar to 'The Needles' off the Isle of Wight."

"Sounds fascinating!" said Sam, sarcastically (not being one given to enjoying physical exercise).

"No, seriously, Sam, you'll enjoy the views once we've got there and the rolling green 'downland' countryside inland will be beautiful too," I stressed.

"Okay, okay, I'll be open minded," she lied, having firmly closed her mind to any potential enjoyment.

We met in reception at ten thirty and set off, Dad and I in the lead with the OS map and camera at the ready. The walk was as spectacular as I had predicted. The view back inland one of tranquillity and gentle rolling contours, out to sea quite breath-taking with a sheer drop of hundreds of feet from clifftop to sea. The wind was light, but I could imagine that on a really windy day any walker would feel the distinct fear of being blasted by an offshore wind over the cliff and into the sea. We sat a safe distance from the end of the promontory and looked out at the four stacks of chalk across the channel. None of us said much, but I took plenty of photos that I knew would generate conversation long after we had finished this holiday. We walked back slowly with the sun rising high into a cloudless blue sky. By one o'clock, we were all back in our hotel rooms with an agreement to meet at three in reception to go down to the beach. The long walk had given us all that wonderful tired feeling where you ache but it somehow feels good. You can't quite decide what to do with your legs but wherever you put them feels restful.

We read, dozed and chatted for a couple of hours, then got ready to go to the beach. Most of the hotel residents were on the beach by the time we arrived, but it was not unduly crowded. I noticed that the Wortmann girls were already in the water. We applied sun-cream and lay on our towels absorbing the sun's heat until it became too much, at which point, Sam and I rushed into the sea and dived headlong into the cold water. At first, it felt great, but it didn't take long for my knees to start going blue. Mum and Dad were knee deep in the sea as we splashed our way back to the beach, dried off and lay down again, eyes closed, to absorb the sun's wonderful rays.

"*Ken ve use zer ball, please?*"

My eyes sprang open to see Heidi and Julia stood in front of us smiling.

"*Naturlich*!" I replied, surprising myself with the instant response. They giggled, grabbed the ball and ran back along the beach throwing it to each other as they went. Sam lay, eyes closed, ignoring the whole event. I lay, eyes closed, trying to

26

stay cool and allow a reasonable time before jumping up and running after them, eager to join in before anyone else did…I lasted about ten minutes!

"Coming, Sam?" I asked, sitting up and quickly scanning the beach for Heidi and Julia.

"No, thanks," came a sleepy reply.

"Well, don't get burned," I warned, half joking and strolled in, what I believed to be, a controlled speed towards them. We played catch, piggy-in-the-middle and splash the catcher in the sea until Julia got bored and re-joined her mother, who was sat comfortably reading her book under a beach umbrella. Mum and Dad had joined Sam so I was free to spend some personal time with Heidi. She swam strongly and talked non-stop. I was completely besotted. Her dazzling blue eyes burned into mine as we spoke, laughed or just looked. She liked pizza, Santana, football, dancing, learning languages, her family, travelling, eating, being on holiday, reading, cinema, swimming, shopping, her friends, TV and radio. She didn't like school, homework, teachers, cooking, washing up, ironing, war, third-world poverty, cruelty to animals or children…or kippers! She had tried them for breakfast during their first week and couldn't cope with the mass of tiny bones. She wasn't sure what she was going to do when she had finished her next year at school. Either go to university or maybe join a big company that wanted her linguistic abilities and travel around the world. Frankfurt, she explained, had a very large airport and airlines were always interested in intelligent young women with language skills. I explained about how I had ended up working in London and that I was currently doing a business studies degree at night school. Heidi seemed impressed but didn't actually say so.

After half an hour or so, we were both getting cold and Heidi said she should re-join her mother and sister. I walked back along the beach to Sam and my parents having first made sure to say, "See you at the dance tonight!"

It was nearly five o'clock and some of the hotel guests had already made their way back up to the garden for refreshments. The fat-faced blonde guy was chatting to the two 'Plain Janes' by one of the large wave breakers. He was sat on the horizontal beam, legs dangling down and swinging. An immediate and cruel image of 'Humpty Dumpty' flashed through my mind and I smiled.

"Booked your dance then?" teased Sam as I sat down on the shingle.

"Maybe," I replied guardedly. "Has anyone found out any more about this dance evening?"

"No," said Mum, "but I overheard some of the other guests enthusing about the last one. Do you think we should have an early dinner to be sure we're finished in time?"

"Good idea, darling," agreed Dad, "I know we all had a good breakfast but after our long walk that seemed a long time ago."

"I'm all for that," confirmed Sam. "How about six thirty? That should give us plenty of time for showers and so on."

We all agreed, packed up our beach things and headed slowly back up the steps to the garden. Musical equipment was being unloaded from vans in the car park and was being carried or wheeled on trollies carefully through the garden into the restaurant area. In the restaurant, waiters were busy rearranging the table layout to accommodate the band.

"Looks very professional," observed Dad as we went into the hotel and through reception. "See you both down here at six thirty."

Back in Room 8, Sam started quizzing me.

"So what great chat-up lines do you use then?"

"Now look," I said defensively, "we just chatted, you know, normally, about likes, dislikes, music, languages, holidays, films and kippers."

"Oh, fantastic! Tell me how you managed a chat-up line with kippers in it!" Sam laughed in disbelief.

"I didn't, you idiot! Heidi just mentioned that she hates them after a battle with one at breakfast last week." I changed the subject quickly. "Do you want first shower or shall I?"

Sam opted for the first shower so I took my book and went out to the garden. It was still warm and I sat in the shade and tried to get into the story. Only a couple of other tables were occupied as most of the guests were doing the same as us and getting ready for an early dinner. At a table near the patio were the families of the two 'Plain Janes' and Humpty Dumpty. I could see where the young man got his looks from as I watched his father getting up to pay Alec for another round of drinks and then, rather carefully, squeezing his considerable bulk back into the rather inadequate garden chair. He looked as if he'd already had a few and was talking loudly to the rest of the group. The band were doing some sound checks and warm-ups in the restaurant in order to be ready and fully set up before dinner started at six thirty. I read until six and then went back to our room. Sam was out of the shower and wrapped from head to toe in towels. She was sat on the edge of her bed with her feet on mine painting her toenails.

"Bet you a tenner that Humpty senior is pissed before the dance starts!" I laughed.

"Who?" asked Sam, looking up from her toes.

"The fat-faced guy's father," I explained and then went on to describe the mental image I had of him on the beach.

Sam giggled. "You are wicked; it's not his fault!"

"Maybe not," I conceded, "but it's fun and it's funny…and his dad looks like he's setting himself up for quite an evening. He was ordering what looked like his third round of drinks at a quarter to six!"

I showered and then selected my most trendy clothes. I was not going to miss a chance to look as good as I could. At twenty past six, we were ready. Sam looked lovely; she had carefully styled her long blonde hair, put make-up on and selected a flattering blouse and skirt. Her red toenails shone out from her glitzy open-toed sandals.

We joined Mum and Dad in reception and went through to the restaurant. Both had dressed up impressively. Dad in a casual but smart jacket and tie and Mum in one of her most expensive outfits. They looked an attractive couple as we went to our table.

The tables had been arranged much closer together to make room for the band to the right of the bar and to provide an area for a few easy chairs where, after eating, guests could sit in between dances or just watch. We were among the first to arrive and chose a table diagonally opposite the band in the far sweep of the big bay window. I kept a careful eye out as the other families arrived, eager to see what Heidi was wearing. Our starters arrived and still no sign of the Wortmann family. We chatted about plans for Monday. Should we go to Corfe Castle and the Blue Pool or go into

Bournemouth to look around the town? We finished our starters and still no sign of Heidi. The restaurant was over half full now and I started to feel a little worried. By now, Mum and Dad had decided to go to Bournemouth the next day to look around the shops. Sam and I wanted to stay flexible and see what the weather was like before making up our minds. We had the car so our indecision wasn't a problem. Just as Alec brought over our main courses, Heidi, Julia and their parents came into the room. They looked over, waved and then made their way to one of the few vacant tables. Heidi looked stunning in a full and lacy white blouse with a flowing checked skirt. Mr and Mrs Wortmann looked very smart, much like Mum and Dad, if perhaps a bit more formal. I relaxed and enjoyed the rest of my meal, looking forward to the dancing.

The 'Dumpties' were sat not far from us at two tables that had been pushed alongside each other to allow two families to sit together. The 'Plains' were sat with them not saying very much and exchanging awkward glances as Dumpty Senior ordered more wine and slapped his wife on the thigh. I winked at Sam and she giggled.

"I do hope that man isn't going to cause a scene!" whispered Mum.

Dad laughed. "I rather hope he is…that would really liven things up!"

"Dad!" hissed Sam. "What about his poor wife?" And she looked sympathetically at Mum.

"Well, it'll be interesting to see who looks 'poor' tomorrow!" And she winked at Sam. It was clear that the women at our table felt that, on balance, Mrs Dumpty was going to come out of this ahead!

We forwent dessert and left the restaurant to enjoy coffees in the garden, where a cool breeze was gently moving the parasols around and the herring gulls were riding the updrafts from the clifftops, calling to each other and looking majestic and menacing at the same time. We finished our coffee and sat back looking at the pinkish blue sky. The musicians from the band were enjoying a last-minute drink at a table nearby before the seven thirty start. I hoped they were going to play some good dancing music, especially some slow, smoochy ones near the end!

"Let's go back in now and save some comfy seats," I suggested.

"Good idea," agreed Sam.

"Dad and I will spend a bit more time out here," said Mum, taking control. "I love to watch the gulls. Why don't you two go in and save us a seat?"

We gladly agreed and went back into the restaurant just as the Wortmann family were coming out. Mr Wortmann gave us his wonderful wide smile and told us that they were going to have a coffee.

I said that we would try to save them some seats, although I had no idea how two of us could save eight seats!

The only table still occupied inside was that of the 'Dumpty-Plains' party. Alec hovered nearby hoping to be able to clear away and get the dance going, but the whole group now appeared lethargic and a bit inebriated. We avoided them and sat down in the easy chairs next to the small dance floor. Sam put her handbag on a vacant seat as a sign of 'reservation'. Alec came over and asked us what we would like to drink.

"What's left?" I asked him, smirking and pointing with my eyebrows over to the Dumpty table.

He laughed. "Aaah, dunnay worry! We've more than they can cope with!"

I ordered a beer and a Bacardi & Coke and watched the band file in and get organised with their instruments and microphones. These people always look so casual with their specialist skill. I'm sure that the reason is they practise and practise so that it looks as if they are being casual…anyway, it worked! They opened with *Moon River*, not a favourite of mine but very well executed, especially as it was purely instrumental. They had obviously done this before because, as if hypnotised by the gentle draw of the music, the entire population of 'The Lymes' garden flowed back into the room.

Sam and I managed to save three seats and Mum and Dad joined us. The Wortmann family arrived just too late and had to find seats elsewhere. The band started up again with *Delilah* and the dance floor was immediately packed with waltzing couples including, I noticed with concern, Heidi and Mr Wortmann. Mum and Dad got up and joined the throng. The Wortmann couple whirled effortlessly around, rising and falling with the beat and looking as if they were straight from *Come Dancing*.

"Oh, shit, Sam," I complained, "I can't do this! What about some disco…or even rock, I can dance to that!"

"Maybe a crash course with Mum…or Dad!" she teased and pointed to them out on the dance floor whirling and bobbing as well. I slouched, sulking, back into my chair and drank my beer wondering what to do next. Dreadful possibilities started to creep into my mind. What if Dumpty Junior could waltz? What if he asked Heidi for the next dance? Sam was right, I should learn as quickly as possible, but I couldn't learn in front of everyone else, not now!

Delilah finished dramatically and all of the waltzers clapped and came off the dance floor. I tried to cheer up and congratulated Mum and Dad on their performance. They were clearly pleased and Dad went off to order some more drinks. The next dance was purely for the young, before they went off to bed, and *The Birdie Song* went down very well. Mercifully, it ended quite quickly. Our fresh drinks arrived and the band started their next number, *Sweet Caroline* by Status Quo. It would not have been my choice, but at least I could move to this. Strangely, no one else made a move for the dance floor so I stayed seated and waited, looking across to Sam and raising my eyebrows to say 'are you up for this?'. She shook her head slowly and then opened her eyes widely, staring hard across the dance floor. Dumpty Senior and Junior were making their way purposefully through the seated waltzers to the dance floor. They stepped into the centre, adopted a serious face-to-face pose, put their thumbs in the tops of their trouser pockets and started moving their upper bodies upwards and backwards, then forwards and downwards. Feet quite still, shoulders working hard back and up, then forwards and down to the beat. They looked ridiculous, but the seated 'waltzers' were smiling and clapping in time. I looked incredulously at Sam, who was nearly crying with laughter. Mum and Dad were clapping too. These people deserved ridicule not encouragement, what was wrong with everyone! The beat got faster and the song seemed to go on and on. Thankfully, it finally ended as Dumpty Senior had tried to take his shirt off over his head and got it stuck because too many of the buttons were still done up. His flabby white flesh was wobbling horribly as he struggled with the resistant garment, but still no comment or condemnation from the crowd, just good-humoured laughter. As they made an unsteady, glassy-eyed exit from the floor further clapping and cheering, the band broke for a quick smoke, refreshments and, no doubt, a good laugh!

I looked around for Heidi and her family. They were sat on the other side of the room nearer to the band and were deep in light-hearted discussion. Mrs Wortmann looked up and caught my eye. I raised my eyebrows as if to say 'Whatever next?'. She giggled and went back to the family discussion. That was pretty much the last contact that I had with the Wortmanns that evening.

Several more ballroom dances were played including a salsa and a foxtrot, followed by a couple of rock numbers. The floor was always packed for the ballroom dances but empty for the rock ones. The Dumpties had retired to their rooms, very wisely, and I was certainly not going to try and follow their act!

Later that night, having sat in my chair the entire evening, I complained to Sam.

"What a disaster! Not a single dance that I could make use of with Heidi."

"Oh, don't worry," Sam sympathised, a bit impatiently, "no one else got near either, apart from her dad. So you haven't lost out."

"Maybe you're right!" I admitted. "But I had such high hopes that it would be a great opportunity."

"Well, stop moaning and go to sleep!" Sam concluded, turning over and abruptly following her own advice.

Monday

I tossed and turned a bit and then succumbed to the sound of the sea and slept until seven thirty the following morning. Once again, the sun shone, the sky was blue and there was a light breeze gently sucking and blowing the semi-closed curtains. I felt hungry and wished that we had arranged to have an early breakfast rather than at eight thirty. Sam was still asleep so I got up, shaved, showered and went out to look at the weather and the sea. No complaints there, both were fantastic. The sky was azure blue with some high wispy cloud, the sea a similar blue with little, white-topped waves tumbling in one after another. Everywhere was quiet. It was Monday morning so no coming or going of guests. I walked down the steps to the beach and sat on the bottom step thinking about what to do today. Corfe Castle and The Blue Pool seemed a better option than Bournemouth shops on such a beautiful day. I hoped that Sam would agree otherwise I'd be on my own for the whole day. I heard footsteps behind me and Sam joined me on the bottom step looking fresh and ready for anything.

"Shopping or sightseeing?" I asked, as neutrally as I could.

"No money for shopping so sightseeing it is," Sam confirmed.

"I'll lend you some money if you really want to go to Bournemouth," I offered. "What do you want to get?"

"No, nothing, thanks," Sam replied. "I want to go to the castle."

We were both hungry so we went back into reception but couldn't wait for Mum and Dad so went straight into the restaurant and ordered our breakfasts. Mum and Dad joined us ten minutes later and took no offence. They were planning a shop route around Bournemouth, which included pub and teashop stop-overs.

"We're going to take my car and go and look at Corfe Castle and The Blue Pool," I confirmed.

"Well, maybe you could take the Wortmann girls with you because we just saw Mr and Mrs Wortmann in reception and they want to come with us to Bournemouth, to buy some things that they saw last week, but the girls don't want to go with them," said Mum.

"Yes, we could," I said, looking at Sam for approval. "When do you think they'll be ready?"

"You're not in a hurry, are you, Paul?" asked Dad. "Why not wait until they're ready and then offer them the option?"

Sam smiled. "We'll wait till they're ready, won't we, Paul?" And she winked at me.

"Yes, of course." My heart pounding, brain racing and wanting to kiss my sister.

We all met up in reception at ten o'clock. The Wortmann family stood all together, quite closely, with Mr and Mrs Wortmann just in front of their two daughters, who looked excited if a little unsure. Mr Wortmann looked a little hesitant and a bit protective of his girls.

"Vill zey be okay?" he asked awkwardly, not asking the question he really wanted to.

"I'm sure they will be fine," I said reassuringly, or I thought it was.

Mr Wortmann still looked doubtful, Heidi and Julia looked a little worried.

Sam rolled her eyes at me and stepped in. "My brother is a very good and very safe driver, Mr Wortmann," she said. "I wouldn't go in the car with him if he wasn't…and I promise I won't let him take his shirt off!"

Mrs Wortmann snorted out a loud laugh, opened her eyes wide in surprise and then quickly covered her mouth with her hand, still laughing. Heidi and Julia bent forward trying to supress giggles but couldn't. Mr Wortmann smiled widely, eventually getting the joke.

"Goot, very goot!" he said, exhaling. "Zen I trust zem wiz you." Mrs Wortmann smiled lovingly at him and took his arm, squeezing it.

So, Dad was driving Mum and Mr and Mrs Wortmann to Bournemouth and I was driving the three girls to Corfe Castle and The Blue Pool. Everyone was happy, especially me. I climbed into the driver's seat, hoping the mini would start first time. Sam got into the front seat and Heidi and Julia got into the back. They were clearly impressed; the mini must be a trendy car in Germany too.

"Zis iz really your car?" asked Heidi, a hint of awe in her voice.

"Yes, it is," I confirmed. "She's rather old and a bit temperamental at times and hasn't been started since Saturday, so don't worry if she takes a few goes to start."

The hot weather had helped and, with no choke, at first turn of the key, she started perfectly…cheers from the back. It was hot already so we rolled down all the windows and drove the twenty minutes towards Wareham and The Blue Pool in reasonable comfort. I asked where they had learned ballroom dancing and Julia replied that it was very common for teenage German boys and girls to learn how to dance that way and that there were many classes that could be attended in Frankfurt. Heidi elaborated that there were twice yearly ballroom dancing competitions, the most important being the 'Silversterball' which was held in a special hall at Frankfurt Zoo on New Year's Eve and that there was a 'warm-up' ball at the end of October for people to dress up and practise. I said that it was sad that we had lost that tradition in England because it looked very graceful.

Sam cast me a sideways glance and raised her eyebrows. I could hear her thinking 'Yes, and a good way to get very close to some good-looking partners!'

We arrived at The Blue Pool, parked and made our way to the signposted vantage point. The combination of the light-coloured Purbeck stone base, the indigenous, colourful algae and the bright blue sky gave the water a wonderful turquoise appearance in contrast to the tall, dark green fir trees that grew right down to the water's edge and completely surrounded the circular lake.

It looked almost unreal! I tried to explain to Heidi and Julia why the water appeared such an amazing colour, but my German and their English couldn't quite stretch to such a complicated subject! So we all took photos instead and accepted the beautiful scenery for what it was without further question. We walked down to the water's edge and then around the sandy edge of the pool.

"Vot dance vos zat funny man doing last night?" asked Heidi, giggling.

Without thinking, I replied, "The Turkey dance!"

"Turkey dance?" repeated Heidi, thinking. "Like an Arabian dance von Turkey?"

Sam giggled. "No, not quite, Heidi," she helped, "Paul calls people that he thinks are idiots 'Turkeys', you know, like the birds that we eat at Christmas, like big chickens!"

"*Truthahne*," I helped further, grateful that, for some strange reason, I could remember my German vocabulary. Screams of laughter came from Heidi and Julia.

"Iz ziss name used often in England?" spluttered Heidi.

"No!" replied Sam. "It's Paul's special word used, more or less, only by him!"

"Turkeys look stupid, sound stupid and move stupidly," I concluded. "The description fits him perfectly!"

Further screams of laughter and impressions of turkeys running madly about from Heidi and Julia. About three-quarters of the way around the pool, we stopped to watch a huge anthill with enormous wood ants swarming over a sticky-looking pine stump and had to make a hasty exit back up the steep slope to the car when it seemed that they had noticed us and started to quick-march in ominously well organised and large columns towards us. Hot and a bit breathless, we sat by the car with all the doors open to let out the heat and laughed at our fear of the ants.

"Paul had a nasty experience with wood ants when we were on a summer holiday in Austria several years ago," began Sam.

"Oh no, Sam," I objected, "don't tell them about that!"

Sam looked over to Heidi and Julia with her eyebrows raised as if to ask 'Do you want to hear the story?'

"Vot happened?" asked Heidi, looking very interested.

"Well," said Sam, enjoying enormously the opportunity to make me look silly, "we had gone up a mountain near Seefeld and had stopped by some woods to enjoy the view and eat our picnic lunch. Paul sat down on a raised mound in the sandy grass and very soon realised that he had some unwanted company!"

I held my head in my hands, but she continued.

"The wood ants were even bigger and more fierce than the ones we just saw and marched straight up Paul's trouser legs, inside has jeans. He felt their big strong feet rather too late and tried to squash them through the denim material, but they fought back and bit him. In the end, he had to take his jeans off to get rid of them!"

Heidi's beautiful blue eyes were wide with mischief now. "Ooh dear," she mocked, "very nasty!"

"Yes, it was," I said defensively. "There were hundreds of them, and they have a painful bite and don't give up when you squish them. I had to escape whirling my jeans over my head to get them out."

Snorts of laughter came from all three girls. Heidi started whirling her hand around and around above her head chanting, 'Go avay, ants. Go avay, ants!' in time with her whirling arm.

Tears were running down Sam's cheeks as she watched, laughing as Heidi took full advantage of making fun of me.

"Thank you, Sam," I said reprovingly. "Very funny story. Now shall we go on to Corfe Castle? It's only about fifteen minutes' drive from here."

My attempt to halt the hilarity failed dismally.

"Check your trousers before you get into the car," warned Sam. "Can't have ants in your pants and drive safely!!!"

Hysterical laughter and falling about from Heidi and Julia...who's understanding of English seemed to be improving much too quickly.

"They don't just bite men, you know," I countered. "I'm not the only one wearing jeans."

Julia sprang up and theatrically whacked the backside of her jeans with both hands. "*Hilfe, Hilfe!*" she shrieked, jumping up and down. "Ants in ze pants!" Heidi shrieked too, sprang up and started chasing after Julia whacking her bottom and shouting, "Got you, got you!"

After a minute or so of this, they were, thankfully, too hot and worn out to keep it up. They sat back down and pretended to hang their heads in shame. They looked up at me with big 'pleading' eyes.

"Ve are zorry," lied Heidi. "No more teasing!"

I inclined my head, smiling. "*Bitte*," I said in mock acceptance of their apology.

We got into the car and set off slowly with the warm breeze blowing in through the open windows. After a minute or so, Heidi and Julia started to squirm around from side to side on the back seat nudging each other.

"I zink ve have zer 'mini' ants back here," joked Julia.

"Well, you'll have to deal with them yourselves." I laughed. "I'm not stopping! We'll be at the castle soon. From the small brochure I got from reception, I'm not sure there's much left of the castle buildings, but apparently, the view from up there is really good."

We arrived, parked, got out of the car and looked up at the remnants of, what had been, a large castle. There was a steep path up to the left of the ruined front of the castle which was, disappointingly, almost all that was still standing. The building appeared to have had three storeys. The empty window openings now only showed a disconnected wall to the right side.

We walked up the steep path to the castle front and could then see that it had been built on top of a very high hill, presumably part of the south downs. The land fell away steeply on all sides around the castle. Clearly, strategically placed to be easily defended should any enemy decide to try and attack. There were a couple of tall joined outer walls made of big slabs of Purbeck limestone with weathered window slits and empty door openings. The disconnected side wall stood entirely on its own, looking as if it would topple over if someone gave it a gentle shove.

We walked up to the ruins, then around them and gazed for a while at the impressive views back towards Swanage several miles away. I took a few photos. It was eleven thirty and we were all hot and thirsty.

"Do you want to have a longer look around?" I asked, hoping the girls would say no.

Heidi and Julia looked at each other, tilted their heads, raised their eyebrows, turned the corners of their mouths down with a shoulder shrug that said 'What do you think?'. Sam agreed that it was time to go back to the hotel and get a cold drink, so we all walked down the hill and got into the hot mini.

"Ver do you go in your car ven you're not on holiday?" enquired Heidi.

"I drive it to the train station, park it, catch the train to London and then drive it home again from the station in the evening." I laughed. "At weekends, I drive it to football matches when I'm playing or go out with my friends to nightclubs or sometimes Sam and I go out into the countryside and find a nice pub. Why do you ask?"

"I vont to learn to drive, and ven I can, I vill go everywhere in my car!" she blurted. "But in Frankfurt, most people take the tram, it's so boring. Iz it hard to learn to drive?"

"For the first few lessons, it is," I replied. "There is so much to remember and so many things to do all at the same time. Which pedal does what, which instruments tell you what and how to steer, look ahead and behind without hitting anything. Getting it wrong can be very dangerous so it is quite nerve wracking. After a while, you start to do the right things without really thinking."

"Paul passed his driving test first time," added Sam, turning and winking to the girls in the back, "but Mum still used to come back from his practice sessions with white knuckles from gripping the seat in terror!" Then she did a very good impression of Mum clamped rigid in the passenger seat, staring fixedly ahead with her body pushed as far back in the seat as possible as if braced for an imminent crash. Snorts of laughter followed from the back seat and I tried not to blush…it was true!

Back at 'The Lymes', we had a refreshing drink in the garden together followed by a light salad lunch and decided to spend the afternoon on the beach.

"I hope they didn't find that too boring," I said to Sam once we were back in our room getting our beach things ready.

"Don't worry. They enjoyed the car ride and a little independence from their parents even if there were only a few bricks and some wood ants to look at!" replied Sam. "They do enjoy a laugh, those two; I like them."

We spent a great afternoon on the beach playing ball, swimming, sunbathing, taking the mickey out of the other guests, counting gulls, knocking down pebble towers and generally enjoying each other's company. At four thirty, Mum, Dad and Mr and Mrs Wortmann joined us. They'd had a great time too and were clearly getting on very well. It had struck me earlier how similar Mrs Wortmann was to my mum in stature, looks, mannerisms and temperament. It seemed a good omen. Back in the garden, we drank tea and talked about tomorrow's games evening. From their experience of the previous week, the Wortmanns were able to tell us that any game from cards to table tennis, tug-of-war to 'blind the children' (Blind Man's Buff) were played on site or there were minibuses to a nearby pub to play skittles or darts. It sounded like virtually the whole hotel got competitive one way or another for one evening. Being a competitive sort myself, I asked what games they had won at last week. Mr Wortmann's eyes twinkled.

"Ve hat vun at zer table game mit money," he boasted, once again showing his infectious, ear-to-ear grin.

"Poker?" I asked, seeking clarification.

"No, no…properties, mit howzes in London," he finished, with a little clap to himself and his family.

"Monopoly," said Sam suddenly.

"Yes, yes," enthused Mr Wortmann, "a vonderful fantasy for uz, a nation of people who rent apartments!"

We all laughed and congratulated them at winning such an English game. We agreed that we would help to pick them a different game tomorrow evening so that they could have a chance to beat the English at another national institution. Heidi explained that they had Monopoly in Germany but that the streets were named after famous German ones.

We'd been so engrossed in our discussions that none of us had noticed dark clouds building out to sea and the wind picking up. After such a hot, still day, we should have expected a storm. Slow rumbles of thunder sounded out to sea like ghostly cannons firing consecutively at each other. We moved inside along with everyone else and watched, almost in awe, as the wind built up quickly, blowing the storm inland. The restaurant, now full of 'five o'clock tea drinkers, was almost pitch black as the huge dark clouds rolled over head. Ten minutes later, sheet lightning suddenly lit the garden and restaurant with a brilliant white light followed almost immediately by a huge thunder clap that shook the room. Small children screamed and cried. Those of us who enjoyed watching the power of nature sat in silence, appreciating the free show and the sudden drop in temperature that would make eating and sleeping much more comfortable. I soon realised that the lights weren't only out in the restaurant…there had been a major power cut.

The storm show continued and the noise from it grew as if we had a full orchestra in the room, crescendoing and leaping, whipping up the senses and emotions of the audience. Rain and hailstones pelted horizontally against the window panes. Young families tried to make their way out of the restaurant to their rooms in the dark, young children still wailing, terrified…but the majority of the guests sat silently, watching. I found myself sitting next to Heidi who was clearly shocked by the sudden power of the storm. She sat rivetted by the dramatic change in the weather, her beautiful blue eyes wide open and apprehensive, her hands gripping her knees, watching the hail and rain forcefully hit the windows and run down in torrents over the window sills. The incredible natural power was as much about the speed and sound as the volume of water and brilliance of the lightning. Slowly and gently, I moved my hand to hers on her knee, and she grasped it gratefully with her other hand. Wave after wave of thunder blasted directly overhead shaking the windows in their frames and rattling glasses on tables. The storm lasted another twenty minutes by which time 'The Lymes' emergency generator had kicked into action. The lights came on abruptly, and Heidi looked a bit embarrassed and released my hand. I smiled at her reassuringly holding her eyes as long as I dared. People looked at each other as if having awoken from a dream. Slowly, quiet conversations began and things got back to normal. Mr and Mrs Wortmann collected the girls and went off to shower and get ready for dinner. We did the same, walking slowly along the corridor to our room. Sam still savouring the thrill of the storm, me still feeling the strong grip of Heidi's hand on mine.

Dinner was a bit of an anti-climax after such a good day but enjoyable nevertheless. The air had cleared and stayed cool after the storm, and as we were all quite tired, we went to bed at ten and slept easily.

Tuesday

At breakfast next morning, Sam asked, "So which games shall we play this evening?"

"It would be good to have a change of scenery," I replied. "I'm up for going out for a game of skittles at the pub."

"Good idea," Sam agreed.

"I'm not sure about bar skittles," said Mum. "We might end up in a smoky old pub all evening with that lunatic from the dance floor!"

"Hhmm, you could be right, dear," agreed Dad, "I would rather stay here and do something that we can walk away from if we want to."

I smiled to myself thinking that an evening with Dumpty Senior in a local skittles pub had plenty of promise for excellent entertainment. Sam clearly had the same thought and said, "Well, we don't all have to do the same thing," and winked at me. "You two can help Mr and Mrs Wortmann win at something here, and we'll take the girls with us to skittles. I doubt that they will be interested in playing Monopoly again…or whist or bridge!"

"Let's ask them what they want to do later on," I suggested.

The weather was windy and a bit overcast so we all decided that a look around Bournemouth shops would be good. Mum was always ready to do some more clothes shopping! Dad drove us there and we walked around the middle-class streets and department stores not really interested in buying anything but killing time just looking. We saw the 'Plain Janes' and the Dumpties doing pretty much the same thing. We acknowledged each other but not much more. Dad bought Mum some perfume and skincare products. Sam bought herself a T-shirt, but I held on to my cash!

The day was brightening up as we drove back towards Swanage, and we planned an afternoon on the beach. Lunch was well underway by the time we got back, and we had a rather hurried, mediocre meal. Dad was all for complaining, but we dissuaded him by emphasising that it had seemed mediocre because it was usually so good and that we should allow them to be less than perfect just this once.

Sam and I went back to our room and prepared for the beach.

"I do hope we get to play skittles with Heidi and Julia tonight," I said. "I can't imagine they'll want to be stuck here and play cards or board games. We proved that we are trustworthy to Mr Wortmann yesterday."

"I'm certain they will want to come," said Sam. "Mum and Dad can look after Kurt and Sylvia and we'll have a laugh with the girls! Heidi seems to be pretty good at getting her own way!"

"Shall we get the minibus or shall I drive?" I asked.

"Let's go on the bus. Then you can have a drink, and we can all take the mickey out of the other guests on the way back!" said Sam.

Once we were ready, we made our way through the breezy garden and down the steps to the beach. The Wortmann family were already there, huddled in a group, throwing pebbles at a pebble tower. The temperature down on the beach was markedly colder than up in the garden, much too cold for swimming, so we walked over, greeted them all and sat down close by.

"Are you going to join us and play skittles tonight, Mr Wortmann?" asked Sam.

I flinched in case he said yes, and I think Mrs Wortmann sensed it because she answered quickly for him.

"Kurt and I vill stay here and play somezing eazy, but if you can be zo kind to take Heidi and Julia, zey vill be happy."

Mr Wortmann looked a bit disappointed, but his wife shot him a very quick, very strong look.

"Can ve go? Pleeease?" begged Heidi excitedly.

"*Ja*, of course!" beamed Mr Wortmann good humouredly.

Heidi beamed at Julia and shot me a quick but intensely bright flash of her beautiful blue eyes. I winked gratefully at Sam. Mrs Wortmann looked pleased with herself too and exchanged an interesting 'knowing' kind of look with Heidi.

We talked about the games that might get played that evening and tried to explain the basics of Cluedo, Trivial Pursuit and various card games. Not surprisingly, equivalent games existed in Germany, and once we had got over the initial difficulties, one of the family would suddenly recognise the game and explain in fast, excited German to the others who would all suddenly get it and smile and nod knowingly. Mum and Dad joined us and suggested that it would be more interesting to stroll along the beach than to sit and get cold whilst demolishing a tower of pebbles. We all agreed and got up and walked north along the beach and almost reached Ballard Point by three o'clock. Mr Wortmann wanted to show his family some of the interesting flora that he had discovered during his earlier walks and they slowly made the long ascent to Ballard Down. Heidi groaned but followed dutifully, casting a despairing glance over her shoulder and doing a rather diminished turkey impression with her arms. Sam and I giggled in appreciation. We strolled slowly back along the beach looking out across Swanage Bay and enjoying the scenery and the fact that we were warmly dressed against the breeze that was blowing steadily inland. Once back at the hotel, we sat in the garden for a while, eyes closed, breathing in the sea air and becoming lulled into a relaxed stupor by the sound of the sea. We dozed peacefully for about an hour. The sound of small children belonging to other guests seeming to get further and further away. When we came to, we ordered the obligatory cups of tea, drank them and returned to our rooms to get ready for the evening…even the best holidays have their routines!

The cost of the skittles evening included pub food, participants only having to pay extra for their drinks. We were to assemble in reception at seven o'clock and arrived bang on time to find that the Dumpties and Plain Janes plus several other families were already gathered there. Hotel staff were busily organising the eight-seater minibus and calculating how many trips it would have to make to get us all to 'The Kings Arms' at Langton Matravers and back. At five past seven, the first group of eight set off.

Langton Matravers is only about two miles from Swanage so the minibus had returned by seven fifteen but there was still no sign of the Wortmann girls. The second party took the minibus whilst we assured the hotel staff that there were at least two more going to join us for the last trip. At twenty-five past seven, Mr and Mrs Wortmann calmly arrived with their daughters, and we wished them luck in whatever they decided to play.

Mr Wortmann looked seriously at me and said, "Zey must not drink alcohol in zer pub."

"Understood and agreed," I confirmed.

He beamed his amazingly wide smile. "Zank you *und viel gluck!*"

We joined the final group outside and the minibus collected us at seven forty. We were inside the pub by ten to eight. The Kings Arms was a good-sized 'country inn' style pub. Wooden floors and tables with a private room at the back with an old wooden skittle ally. One of the hotel staff had come with the first group, and she was busily ushering the skittle teams through the saloon bar into the back room where there were two large tables pushed together with sandwiches, pork pies, scotch eggs, crisps, nuts, pickled onions and chips laid out ready. There was also a small bar which was, by now, pretty besieged by thirsty 'Lymes' guests. I noticed that Dumpty Senior was already well into his first pint and gave Sam a nudge, nodding in his direction.

"I do hope he has a skinful tonight!" I whispered. "It was so entertaining last time."

"As long as you promise to make sure that we're not in the same minibus going back." She giggled.

The girls gathered plates, knives, forks and serviettes, and Sam tried to explain what the various plates of food were. Scotch eggs and pickled onions seemed a particular problem for Heidi and Julia to appreciate and they couldn't understand why Sam cringed when they covered their chips with mayonnaise. I had taken the drinks order and was queuing patiently at the bar. I had accepted Heidi's fervent request for 'beer please' and hoped I wouldn't upset her parents by getting half a lager for her. The lady from the hotel was trying to organise us into teams and was randomly handing out pre-prepared cards with a letter and number on them. I got A6, Sam was B3, Julia A3 and Heidi got B4. We quickly realised that this meant we were not all going to be in the same team. There were similar concerns elsewhere in the room and a mad bargaining and card swapping frenzy started. Finally, after buying two un-budgeted drinks, I managed to get us all into Team B. The hotel lady looked amused at all this activity and had obviously seen it happen many times before. She carried on with her job and handed out slips explaining the rules and etiquette of the game. Two balls thrown one after the other to try and knock down all ten skittles. Player A1 went first then B1 then A2, etc. The fallen skittles were to be re-set by a player from the opposing team, whilst the person who has just bowled retrieves the wooden balls for the next player.

Team B included us four plus the Plain Janes, Dumpty junior and his mum plus some others that we recognised but hadn't met before. Once the eating was over, each team began to group together, check that there was a common understanding of the rules and joke and jeer at the other team. Play was to start at eight forty-five and finish no later than ten thirty. Jill, we found out her name at last, from the hotel was scoring. The room was quite hot now, and I enjoyed watching Heidi take her sweatshirt off over her head to reveal a tight-fitting pink t-shirt. We were all red-cheeked and raring to go. Last minute drinks were bought and then play commenced.

Player A1 started. Unlike ten pin bowling, there was no gully either side of the alley, and we quickly learnt that bouncing the ball off one side could be a good idea when only a few skittles were left 'trapped' on the opposite side. It also seemed beneficial if serious spin was applied to the hard, wooden ball since it helped it to crash from one skittle to another without losing much speed.

Team A cheered as A1 scored seven. B1, Dumpty junior, scored eight, much to his delight. As the game progressed, we were impressed by the relatively high scoring, but no one had yet managed all ten, let alone a 'strike'. Sam knocked down six and Heidi got nine, too much cheering and whooping from me! Then it was Dumpty Senior's go! He stood at the end of the alley gripping the ball tightly, red-faced, with his shirt untidily untucked on one side. He took a long look down the alley, hauled his body slowly up, pulling his right arm far behind him then quickly down and forward as he stomped his foot in front and bowled the ball as fast and hard as he could at the centre skittle. The ball was not perfectly spherical and it was going so fast that it took a little hop just before connecting with the body of the skittle. It glanced sharply upwards, just clipped the left of the belly of the centre skittle and flew over the rest of them, crashing into the 'ditch' at the back. Howls of laughter accompanied the astonished look on his face as the centre skittle rocked back and forth before finally gently resting back into an upright position. He tried to appeal for a 're-rack' and a 'proper' ball but was shouted down by Team B followed by a calm ruling from Jill the umpire. Jill said that it had to count as his first ball the same as it would for anyone else. His face narrowed, not easy for someone with such fat jowls, and he frowned a dark frown, collected his second ball and without much preparation bowled it. This time, he rather over-compensated for his initial mistake and bowled it far too slowly for it to do much damage, resulting in a score of five. He walked sulkily down the alley and bowled the two balls back up. I was next up and was determined not to make the same mistakes. I had noticed one of the earlier bowlers put heavy side spin on the first ball with a good result and I did my best to do the same. The ball cannoned off the side of the centre skittle, knocking it down, stayed in contact with the alley floor and spun off strongly, knocking another five skittles over. I looked across to Heidi, Julia and Sam, smiled and winked, gently throwing the second ball up and down in my right hand as if waiting to catch the remaining four skittles off guard. I carefully took aim, took a deep breath and bowled fast, spinning the ball as I threw it. The ball ploughed into the left-hand side of the most forward skittle sending it crashing into the three behind it. They all ended up spinning slowly on their sides on the alley floor. Sam, Heidi and Julia and all of Team B cheered and clapped. I inclined my head slightly in acceptance of their adulation and went to fetch the balls. I re-joined the girls and took their praise gratefully. Heidi gave me a little punch on the arm and a wonderful, bright-eyed smile.

The evening continued well with all members of our team scoring respectably and despite a strike from Dumpty Senior on his second go, we won by ten points. The game over, Jill rang for the minibus and groups of eight went out slowly through the pub, discussing the finer points of the game, to the car park and caught the minibus back to the hotel. We were in the last group, which included the Plain Janes. One of the daughters asked me if I had played skittles before because she was very impressed with my high scoring. I replied that I had played ten pin bowling before, but that it was quite different, being far more accurate and predictable, so my high scores were probably just luck. I was about to carry on the conversation when I noticed Heidi's face set in a scowl, looking directly at the girl in a kind of challenge, so instead I finished along the lines that I thought that the whole team had played well and certainly deserved to win. The minibus arrived, and we all boarded. Heidi and Julia sat together, deep in German conversation, talking so fast that I couldn't understand. I sat next to Sam and tried to make casual conversation about what we could do the next day.

"I think that Heidi got a bit jealous when that other girl started talking to you in the car park," teased Sam when we got back to the hotel.

"Maybe," I speculated, "or maybe she was just a bit tired." Privately, I took this as a good sign and reflected that it had been a good evening all around. Mum and Dad had already gone to bed so we went back to our room, read a while, then slept soundly as usual, lulled by the gentle sound of the sea.

Wednesday

Wednesday morning was fine and sunny, and Sam and I tried to think of new outdoor activities that we could enjoy so as not to get bored of the beach. After breakfast, we asked at reception what else the hotel had to offer and were a little disappointed that the sum-total seemed to be some old bicycles that guests could borrow and maybe use to go on a picnic. Sam wasn't keen, she didn't enjoy physical exercise and thought that cycling around country lanes would be positively dangerous. In the hope of convincing her more, I asked if we could see the bikes. Alec was sent for and took us to a small garden shed tucked away behind some of the tall pine trees on the far side of the car park.

"You'll not be impressed, I'm afraid," he ventured in his broad Scottish accent, fiddling with the rusty old padlock. "I cannot remember the last time these bikes saw the sun!"

"I'm sure they can't be that bad," I replied positively. "How many are there?"

"We're about to find out!" wheezed Alec as he forced the padlock free and pulled open the door. A stale smell of cobwebs, dust, lawnmower fuel and wood stain drifted out and we all peered into the gloom.

"After you, Alec," I said unhelpfully, gesturing to the shed.

In he went and after some muffled crashing about appeared with a rusty old bike with a cobweb-filled basket on the front. The frame must, at one time, have been red but was now a dull brown. The saddle was dusty and looked a bit frail. The handlebars were rusty and had an old bell attached to the left-hand side. The tyres were both flat.

Alec went back in and brought out a similar machine, this time with a frame that must have started life white. Two more trips resulted in a motley selection of four bikes, one with no handlebars at all.

"This one is for the more advanced cyclist!" joked Alec. Sam and I laughed out loud and I went to assess the roadworthiness of them more closely.

"I'll go and get some cloths to clean them up with," volunteered Alec, hurrying back towards the hotel.

"Don't worry on my account," Sam shouted after him. "There's no way I'm getting on any of them!" And she went back to the hotel to read leaving me alone with the rusty wrecks, my optimism slightly dented.

Alec soon returned with cloths, a bucket of water, some car wash and a bicycle pump. He and I got busy and soon established that one bike had punctures to both front and rear tyres. Fortunately, the other two 'good ones' seemed reasonably functional, if not pretty, even after some rigorous cleaning.

"I'll leave them propped up against a table in the garden to dry off," Alec offered helpfully.

"Cheers, and thanks for your help," I replied.

I went back to the room and found Sam lying lazily on her bed, deep in her book.

"Well, two of the bikes do work," I reported.

Sam put her book down. "What a shame that only two can go cycling!" she observed. "I wonder who you can persuade? It won't be me!"

We walked around to reception and found Mum and Dad waiting there.

"Ahh, there you are, did you find something new to do today?" asked Dad.

"Paul's going cycling and I haven't decided yet," answered Sam. "What about you?"

"Mum would like to go to Corfe Castle and The Blue Pool and then come back for lunch. Depending on the weather, we may just relax and read this afternoon," advised Dad. "Where are you getting a bike from?"

"Oh, the hotel has a couple of them that can be borrowed," I confirmed. "Alec just helped me clean them up a bit. But it does rather split us up, doesn't it? Do you mind?"

"Not at all," replied Sam quickly. "You won't get me on one of those things for love, nor money. I think I'll go and read on the beach."

"Okay, I'll go and see if any of the Wortmanns would like to go for a cycle," I said, ignoring a knowing look between Sam and Mum, and I walked off into the garden.

The Wortmann family were seated at a table resting after a late breakfast. They seemed to be talking about the itinerary for the day as I arrived.

"Good morning, everyone," I began. "The hotel has two bicycles that guests can borrow. None of my family want to go and I wonder if any of you would like to join me for a cycle ride today?"

Julia looked at Heidi. Heidi raised her eyebrows and looked at her mother. Mr Wortmann was already looking intently at his wife. Mrs Wortmann smiled at me and said, "Zey only have two zycles?"

"Only two that are safe to ride, I'm afraid, and Sam isn't interested in cycling," I replied truthfully.

"Ahh, hmm," said Mrs Wortmann thinking. "Zycling is not common in Frankfurt, people walk or take a tram."

"I can ride a zycle," chipped in Heidi quickly, "I learned at school."

"I know you can," agreed her mother sympathetically, "but you don't zycle often and here are cars and motorbikes on small lanes. Iz zer a lane for zycles, Paul?"

"Er, no, not a separate cycle lane," I admitted, "but there are some quiet country lanes with very little traffic, and I hadn't intended to go very far or for very long, just a couple of hours maybe."

The tension on Mrs Wortmann's face eased a little.

"If Heidi would like to come, I will make sure that I cycle behind her so that any car approaching from behind will see me and go around me first," I added.

It took a while for Mr and Mrs Wortmann to understand, but I demonstrated the principle on the table with some coins that I had in my pocket. They looked at each other, clearly wanting to discuss without anyone else present, but since that was not possible, Mr Wortmann relented.

"Okay zen," he conceded. "Ven vill you leave and get back?"

It was around ten o'clock so I promised, "If we leave at about ten thirty, I will be sure to have Heidi back here by one o'clock at the latest."

Mr Wortmann looked at his wife, she paused, then nodded slowly, clearly still not really happy about this. Heidi looked from one parent to the other with beseeching eyes.

"Zen one o'clock iz zer 'd time'," said Mr Wortmann very seriously, looking straight into my eyes so that there was no doubt he meant it.

"Yes, of course, Mr Wortmann," I agreed. "One o'clock deadline to have Heidi back here."

Heidi beamed and got up from her seat. She hugged both her mum and dad. Julia looked at bit dejected, but Mr Wortmann offered her the use of some of his camera equipment for the morning and she cheered up instantly.

"Show me the zycles please," urged Heidi.

We walked purposefully around to the side of the garden where Alec had left the bikes to dry off. Heidi couldn't stifle a laugh when she saw them.

"You can have the one with the basket," I offered.

She tried it out for size. The saddle squeaked loudly as she sat on it, making her jump. Her feet reached the ground easily making it look pretty safe. She held the handlebars and tried the brake grips.

"No problem," she said seriously and squeezed the trigger of the bell. Nothing happened. We looked at each other and waited in anticipation, still nothing.

"It's stuck," I concluded and gave it a sharp tap with my knuckles...nothing.

Heidi pushed off and had a practice cycle in a large circle around me. She seemed quite proficient.

"Try the brakes please," I asked.

She pulled on both brake levers and the bike squeaked and shook noisily to a halt.

Heidi dismounted triumphantly and lent the bike back against the table. We had just turned to walk away when the bell gave a faint single 'ting'. Single 'tings' continued getting gradually louder and closer together until the trigger had worked its way back to the start point. I looked at Heidi with a grin and said in a stupid Irish accent, "Now der's a strange ting!"

"Der's a strange ting?" she repeated, frowning, then she burst out laughing as she got the joke.

"Silly." She giggled and punched my arm.

We went back to find the Wortmann family who were still sat at the same table and had clearly had the discussion that they had wanted to have earlier.

"How iz zer zycle?" Mr Wortmann asked Heidi seriously "Iz it safe?"

"It iz zer right size and has a basket and a bell," she replied, equally seriously.

"Paul, you vill look after our Heidi carefully," he said, staring deep into my eyes and then, "ve vill have her back safely."

"Yes, Mr and Mrs Wortmann." I looked from one to the other. "I will take great care of Heidi."

They stood and we shook hands as if making some kind of contract.

Heidi and I went to my car and I got my OS map. I spent fifteen minutes planning a circular route starting from

Swanage, west through the little villages of Acton and Worth Matravers, across Kingston and Harman's Cross then Corfe Castle and back east along Woolgarston and into Swanage. It looked to be only about ten miles, but I reckoned that there would be some fairly steep hills and the bikes didn't look very speedy. We returned to the Wortmann family and showed them the route. Mr and Mrs Wortmann seemed reassured once they could see that we would not be cycling on anything but the smallest country roads. Mrs Wortmann said something quickly in German to Heidi that sounded pretty serious and then wished us a 'Good zycle'. Julia looked a bit envious as we walked away to get our bikes. As we pushed them through the car park towards our journey's start, I realised that I hadn't tried out the 'white' bike and so got onto it before reaching the road. The frame was rather small and my knees seemed to come up rather high when I peddled. The saddle squeaked with every movement, the chain clanked and the brakes screamed when applied…but the tyres were still full of air and it worked. Heidi was already laughing as she got onto her bike and immediately pulled the bell trigger…the single 'tings' started slowly, getting gradually faster and continued as we turned left out of the hotel towards Langton Matravers and Acton. We were both still laughing at the cacophony of noises coming from the bikes when we had completed the first mile, but the effort of pedalling soon made us fall into silent effort, me keeping a close watch on Heidi ahead of me in case she drifted too far into the centre of the road. There were high hedges either side making it difficult to see what traffic was approaching, but we reached Langton Matravers without seeing a car or motorbike.

"Zis zycle vill not vin a race!" shouted Heidi, standing out of the saddle on the pedals to help her up the steep incline. She was wearing a tight white T-shirt and tight blue jeans and I was enjoying the view from my position as 'guard'.

"Never mind, all looks great from here!" I joked.

Heidi turned to grimace over her shoulder at me, wobbled badly and rode over a drain cover causing her to veer temporarily into the centre of the road. She shrieked and then burst out laughing, quickly steering back to the side.

"Don't you make me crash!" she shouted. "My mother von't forgive you!"

The joke had a large element of truth which made me worry for a moment. We passed 'The Kings Arms' pub and Heidi waved at it, wobbling badly again shrieking and then, re-gaining control, laughing. She certainly was enjoying herself.

"In two miles, we need to turn left and head towards Acton," I shouted. "We should get a good view of the sea from there."

Heidi rang her bell in anticipation, the 'tings' were now getting quicker and closer together as the spring inside was getting used to moving again.

In ten minutes, we reached the junction and followed the sign left to Acton, heading due south towards the coast. We enjoyed the fact that the road was now flat and had better visibility ahead so we could ride side-by-side. We were both quite hot so stopped at a small, white-washed village store and I bought us each a coke. We sat on a bench and relaxed for a moment, watching as a few local people milled around the small parade of shops. Several other cyclists went past heading the other way.

"*Brost!*" said Heidi, bashing her bottle against mine and taking a deep swig. "Zanks for zer zycle!" And then she burped loudly.

"Charming!" I laughed. Heidi blushed, turned to me and punched my arm like she'd done before. She caught my gaze and held it for a long moment, her dazzling blue eyes wide and inviting. My turn to blush. I looked at my watch, we had been gone for half an hour and not even covered a quarter of the route.

"We had better get going again if we're not to be back late," I warned.

"Okay," said Heidi putting the cap back on her bottle and tossing it into the basket on the front of her bike.

We set off again slowly, cycling side-by-side and looking ahead to the coastal plain and the sea. The road bent suddenly right and we continued for a couple of miles to Worth Matravers.

"Why don't many people cycle in Germany, Heidi?" I asked.

"It's only in zer big cities like Frankfurt," she replied, "zer are stony streets and tram lines zo it is very difficult on a zycle, but in small places like zis, zey probably do. It's so beautiful here," she finished.

"It is in summer," I agreed, "but in winter, it's probably a bit grim. Cold and wet with nothing to do."

"Does it snow here in vinter?" asked Heidi.

"Not much here on the south coast," I answered, "but there's quite a lot in the north of England and in Scotland. What about in Frankfurt?"

"A lot, especially in zer mountains nearby," she replied.

We stopped briefly in Worth Matravers to look out over St Alban's Head to the sea. The village was an almost exact carbon copy of Acton with white-washed thatched cottages, a small shopping parade with a telescope pointing out to sea.

"Iz it like zis where you live?" asked Heidi.

"No." I laughed. "Nothing like this at all. There are lots of streets with many brick houses in each, large shopping areas, no sea but a big river, a motorway and an airport nearby. So it's much noisier, busier, more people and cars. It's not part of a big city like Frankfurt, but it is a sort of continuation of London because many small towns grew up by the River Thames and they all linked together to give almost continuous population. In the car, if the traffic isn't bad, it only takes thirty minutes to drive from my parents' house into London. I guess it's about twenty miles away."

"Frankfurt has a river alzo," said Heidi. "It's called zer Main. It is huge, dirty and polluted. It brings zings for industry, but iz not good for animals or fish. It brings money not life."

I looked at my watch again. It was eleven fifteen and I knew we needed to get a move on.

"Heidi, if we are to get back on time, I need you to get back on that speed machine and get your lovely legs pushing those pedals around pretty quickly!" I urged.

She looked slowly around at me with just a hint of a smile.

"And vot is zo lovely about my legs?" she teased.

I hadn't intended to make things quite so obvious, but since I had, I could see no way back.

"Heidi, it's not just your legs…all of you is lovely, your hair, your face, the way you smile, your deep blue eyes, the way you laugh, your figure…everything."

We were sat very close on the dry, chalky ground. Seagulls screeched out to sea. The sun was bright and we squinted into each other's eyes and then she leant over, kissed me quickly on the lips, got up and found her bike.

"Ver ve go next?" She giggled. *Good question!* I thought.

We left Worth Matravres and headed north towards Corfe Castle along a very quiet minor road, again with high hedges either side holding in the heat. The road was fairly level and we made good progress, turning left towards Kingston in just ten minutes. From Kingston to Corfe Castle was a hard climb, but as we turned right and cycled down a tiny road in the direction of Woolgarston, the journey was all downhill. We had made good time and it now seemed that we could be back by twelve thirty. We free-wheeled much of the way, Heidi holding her legs out either side of the bike and whooping. I tried to dissuade her since there were still cars around and I couldn't let her have an accident.

Woolgarston was another picture postcard village and we free-wheeled through eventually turning right to head back to Swanage. We crossed a railway line. Having waited five minutes for a train to pass and the crossing gates to rise.

"Vot time is it?" asked Heidi.

"Ten past twelve," I shouted back.

"Ve vill be back early," she replied.

"Probably," I agreed, "but at least your mother won't hit me!"

"She likes you," said Heidi. "She just zeems strict zomtimes."

"She reminds me of my mum," I said, "she has very similar mannerisms."

"Manner vot?" queried Heidi, slowing down and stepping off her bike.

"Mannerisms," I repeated, "ways of saying things, the way she makes her face show what she's thinking. The way she moves and expresses things with her hands. She has a good sense of humour too."

We had plenty of time so we pushed our bikes back from the road, past a gap in the hedge and into a field. The heat was stifling, no air was moving at all; it was like stepping off a plane into a middle-eastern country. We left our bikes on the ground and laid on our backs, knees bent, faces to the sun and eyes closed. With my arms relaxed by my side, I could have easily gone to sleep, but then I felt Heidi's hand grip mine. Our fingers entwined. Neither of us said anything, we just lay there…in touch.

"Do you have a boyfriend in Germany?" I asked bravely.

"If I had one, vood I kiss him?" Heidi replied vaguely.

"Well, yes," I supposed.

"Zen I don't have one now," she concluded, "and you?"

"No, I don't have a boyfriend either!" I replied.

She sat up and squinted at me, smiled and punched my arm. "Silly." She giggled.

She lay back down, took my hand again and we rested. After a while, I checked my watch.

"Heidi, we need to go back to the hotel," I whispered.

"Not yet," she protested.

"We need to be back by one like I promised, otherwise your parents will be angry," I continued.

"Ve have time to stay longer," she objected.

We lay for another five minutes, but then, I had to insist.

"Heidi, we really must go now please."

She let go of my hand. "Okay, okay. Let's go zen," she huffed and got up, got onto her bike and started to cycle before I could say anything more. I mounted my bike quickly and caught up with her. We cycled quickly back to the hotel and saw both of our families waiting in the garden. Heidi put her bike by the shed and went to join her parents and Julia. I carefully put mine alongside and joined Mum, Dad and Sam at their table. Heidi waved across at me, smiling broadly as she sat down and started to tell her parents about the bike adventure. I heaved a huge sigh of relief inside and started to tell my family about the morning.

Twenty minutes later, Mr Wortmann came over smiling and thanked me for looking after 'his Heidi' and then they all went off for a late lunch.

Back in our room later, Sam probed, "So how did it really go then?"

"Pretty good," I answered, "I think we're getting on very well."

"Heidi seemed in a bit of a mood when you got back," Sam continued.

"Oh, she just wanted to stay out for longer, but I insisted that we get back on time so as not to upset her parents. She's very strong willed and used to getting her own way I think, but I'm sure that she enjoyed herself."

The sky had darkened and clouded over and the wind was picking up by the time we met Mum and Dad in the garden. We decided it would be a good idea to have a look around Poole. Dad drove and we arrived in Poole just after two o'clock. The cloud cover remained, but there was no sign of any rain. We parked and found a Tourist Information kiosk and got a detailed street map of the old town. The walk started on the quay by Poole Pottery, which we walked slowly around first, admiring the intricate pottery items and graphic design work. Mum was particularly interested, being a bit of a 'potter' herself. We followed the tourist trail looking out for the brass plaques to guide us to places of interest, many of which seemed to be pubs with colourful histories. Across the quay, we could see many boatyards where hideously expensive, sleek power boats were being crafted. The name 'Sunseeker' was everywhere. As we walked further around the quay, Sam particularly appreciated the beautiful 'Sea Music' sculpture by Sir Antony Caro. Then more pubs and some information about the part that Poole Harbour played in the D-Day embarkations to Normandy to rescue the allied forces trapped on the northern French coast in the Second World War.

The Customs House was impressive and elegant as was the Mansion House. We followed the map route past several churches to the Guildhall then past several more pubs ending at the Waterfront Museum, which gave us a quick recap of the history of Poole. It was now four o'clock and we sat outside the Kings Head pub enjoying a refreshing drink and debating what to do next. We settled for a short cruise around the harbour and enjoyed the fantastic views looking out over Studland Bay, around past Brownsea Island Nature Reserve and across towards Swanage before returning to the quay.

The walk, the salty air and the gentle motion of the boat made us all rather sleepy, and I was glad that Dad was driving us back to the hotel. We arrived back at the hotel at around six and went to our rooms to shower and get ready for dinner.

"I'm starving!" complained Sam. "All that walking and sight-seeing has made me really hungry."

"Me too," I agreed, "and you didn't go for a two-hour bike ride this morning,"

"Well, who insisted on going? And we all know why!" She laughed.

"You're right," I conceded. "The effort was well worth it. I'll tell you more after we've eaten."

We went to the restaurant bar to have a drink and wait for Mum and Dad. Alec was there as usual and beamed at me.

"How did you get on this morning?" he asked, eyebrows raised and with a twinkle in his eyes. "The bikes held out well despite the steep hills and uneven roads," I confirmed.

"That's not quite what I meant," he replied with a wink and nodded in the direction of a table in the restaurant where the Wortmann family were just settling themselves. "Was your wee lassie okay?" he whispered semi-secretly, winking again. "All progressing well? She's quite a beauty!"

"All going well, thanks, Alec." I grinned. "Thanks again for your help with the bikes."

"Anytime, anytime." He beamed and got our drinks just as Mum and Dad were arriving at our usual table. We had an uneventful but delicious dinner and retired to our rooms. I talked Sam through all that had happened during the cycle ride and she agreed that there was the potential for something good to come of it.

Thursday

As we made our way towards breakfast the following morning, we were aware of a lot of unusual activity. The reception area was cordoned off by official-looking burgundy ropes threaded through gleaming chrome stands. 'NO ENTRANCE' signs were strung along them.

Alec was there looking flustered, trying to re-direct hungry residents in a friendly way towards the restaurant for their breakfasts via a new route.

"What's happening, Alec?" I enquired smiling.

He looked at me in a rather despairing way. Clearly, I wasn't the first to ask him that question and he was a bit fed up a having to repeat himself!

"Oh man!" He grimaced. "We've a delivery of new machines for the residents – you know, gaming machines, a fruit machine with a £50 jackpot and a special new video game. They have to be moved in very carefully so as not to disturb the software. No bumps or bruises if you get my drift!"

"Oh, okay," I replied, interested. "Sounds like quite a new thing for the hotel."

"You bet!" he agreed. "Not everyone is keen, but the top brass think it will show that 'The Lymes' is right up to date with the latest gizmos!"

"Well, we'll look forward to making a few small investments ourselves once they're safely in," I confirmed, being quite keen on a little flutter on a fruit machine and enjoying a good video game as long as it wasn't too complicated. Sam and I often happily spent a few quid on these machines in our favourite pub.

"Sounds good, Alec," agreed Sam. "We'll form an orderly queue once they're in place. Good Luck!"

"Thanks very much." Alec grinned, relaxing a bit. "I may need it!"

These new arrivals were the talk of the breakfast room as residents took the short detour and watched big, strong delivery men manoeuvring the tall, heavy, bubble-wrapped machines from the car park into the hotel on 'removal-men' type trollies.

"Well, I don't know about this," worried Dad. "I hope this won't mean hordes of crazed gamblers blocking up reception and making a lot of noise all day and night."

"Don't worry, dear," soothed Mum, "I'm sure that the hotel directors have done their homework and are just hoping to add some new interest for some of those inclined to waste their hard-earned money in those machines." She cast me a quick sideways glance. "I fear that once the residents realise that those type of machines are programmed to win and deliver the hotel a profit, they won't get used very much."

We finished our breakfasts and were disappointed to see that the weather forecast had been right. Dark, rain-laden clouds were blowing in from the sea and it was already drizzling. Sam and I left our parents having a final coffee and discussing their plans. We walked back towards reception. Alec was still there directing operations. The two tall, sparkling new machines were now stood against the wall with enough gap between them to allow players at each to enjoy their game without players on the other machine being able to watch how or what they were doing. The electronic display screens were now lit up with bright, colourful flashing lights and the sound systems were being tested. Alec was asking the 'engineers' to turn the volumes down so that the reception staff could still do their jobs without getting a headache! He rolled his eyes at us and shrugged his shoulders. He clearly hated the personal responsibility for having these controversial pieces of modern, high-technology equipment installed. We stood and watched a moment more and then started off towards our room. Sam suddenly stopped and looked at me, listening intently to something.

"Dig-Dug!" she shouted, and instantly, I too could hear the intro music of our favourite video game playing quietly from one of the machines.

"Wow," I agreed. "It is! Fantastic!"

We turned and walked back to see the familiar game start-screen with our favourite hero, Dug, in his white uniform ready to dig tunnels down into the earth and fire his harpoon into any monster or dragon that he found and then pump it up with his foot pump until it exploded! We'd had many happy hours learning how to successfully navigate through each, ever more difficult, level, remembering the secrets of each one – where to dig, which way to go when being chased by two monsters and how to trick them to their doom by impaling them on the harpoon and then foot-pumping them up to explode! We'd rather not admit the amount of money that we'd spent to gain the knowledge we had and kept it to ourselves.

"Spot on, Alec." Sam laughed. "This is our favourite!"

"Really?" queried Alec. "Is it that good?"

"Oh yes," I confirmed. "Highly addictive and very entertaining."

"What level have you reached?" asked the engineer.

"Ah, that's for us to know and to improve upon," said Sam evasively.

"Okay." He laughed and turned to Alec. "All done."

Alec shook his head, smiling, clearly happy that they had delivered a highly valued game. We went back to our room and started going through our change to make sure that we saved as many 10p, 20p and 50p coins as possible ready for a Dig-Dug session later on.

"What shall we do now?" wondered Sam aloud.

"Maybe there's a cinema somewhere near. I haven't seen a film for a while," I replied.

We went back to reception and asked.

"There is a kind of cinema in the Grand Hotel in Swanage," confirmed the receptionist and she helpfully called them to ask what was showing. "They have *Jaws 2* on at two thirty today," she advised. "You'll need to get there by at least two as there will probably be a lot of people wanting to go on a day like this."

"Sounds good," I said hopefully, looking at Sam.

"Hmmm," she said pensively, "I saw the original *Jaws* and liked it, but I'm not really one for sequels. It might be a poor second version with a weak storyline."

"It has most of the original cast," I enthused, "I'll bet they have improved some of the special effects – you know, learnt from the first film. I'm keen to go."

"Okay, me too," agreed Sam. "Shall we ask Heidi and Julia if they want to come?"

"Fine by me." I smiled. "But you knew that!"

It was now eleven thirty and we went back to reception on our way to see where our parents were. The Wortmann family were gathered around one of the new machines which were now fully operational and using their flashing lights and music to full effect to lure in inquisitive passers-by.

"Hi, Paul und Sam." Mr Wortmann beamed. "Vot about deez?"

"Good fun, I'm sure," I replied, "Sam and I have played that game before in a local pub."

"Iz it hard?" asked Heidi.

"You just have to know what to do." Sam smiled. "Paul and I have enjoyed that game many times."

"Zo you can show us?" joined in Julia.

"Later on we'd be glad to," I confirmed. "Shame about the weather."

"Ve vill go to Poole I zink," said Mrs Wortmann.

"Again," blurted Heidi sulkily, obviously not in favour.

"Vot else can ve do?" replied her mother, a little irritated.

"Well, we may go to see a film this afternoon," I said helpfully. "There's a screen in The Grand Hotel in Swanage apparently."

"Vot film vill play?" enquired Mr Wortmann.

"*Jaws 2*!" hissed Sam in a menacing voice.

Heidi and Julia looked at each other, eyebrows raised in hope. Mr and Mrs Wortmann exchanged a knowing glance too.

"Zis film zownds scary," Mr Wortmann ventured. "Iz it okay for zees girls?"

"Oh yes!" I said casually. "It's a PG, which means parental guidance, so any child over twelve can go if their parents agree. Did you see the original *Jaws* film?"

"Not allowed," huffed Heidi, "zu young!"

"Oh well, that was at least two years ago," I said hurriedly. "This one will be no worse than that. Sam and I saw it, and it was exciting but not terrifying. Not too much blood."

Mr and Mrs Wortmann discussed in German. I caught bits of what they said about age and sleeping but not much else. Soon Heidi and Julia were involved too. The discussion ended with Heidi and Julia smiling so I guessed they had been given permission.

"If you vill take zem, zey can go." Mrs Wortmann smiled. "If zey don't zleep vell, zat iz for zem to vorry!"

Heidi and Julia looked pleadingly at me.

"Yes, of course, we'd be delighted to take them with us," I confirmed.

All was arranged. We met in reception at one thirty, and I drove us into Swanage. I parked in the Grand Hotel car park. There were only a few spaces left so I guessed that people were arriving already for the film. We went into the rather posh hotel lobby through some old but very well kept dark wooden swing-doors with smear-free windows and gleaming brass edging. Sam went over to the reception desk to ask about the film. There were several large, floor-standing posters advertising *JAWS 2* with a big picture of a young lady water-skier smiling happily towards us, oblivious of the huge, menacing, open-mouthed shark towering out of the water behind her. Heidi nudged Julia, pointing at the poster. Julia looked nervous but smiled.

Sam returned. "We have to take the lift to the second floor," she advised. "We pay there too."

We took the lift to the second floor, and I went over to the small, dark, circular wooden kiosk. It was in the same style as the front doors, old fashioned but gleaming with properly leaded windows all around. There were dark wooden panels extending either side of the kiosk across the room to prevent anyone from just walking in without paying. I paid for all four of us despite objections from Heidi, who had been given money by her father for herself and Julia. We went through the small door into a waiting area with several small kiosks selling drinks, sweets and popcorn. Having recently had lunch, we passed on those offerings and waited in a queue with around thirty other people to be let into the 'screen-room'.

At ten past two, a couple of cutely uniformed usherettes opened the doors to the screen room, and we all went into the little cinema. There were traditional cinema-style upholstered seats with fold down bottoms. I made sure that Sam went in first, then me, then Heidi and lastly Julia. By two thirty, the little cinema had an audience of around a hundred and fifty and was almost full. The lights went down. There were adverts and trailers for up-coming films like *The Deer Hunter*, *The Boys from Brazil*, *Grease* and *Heaven Can Wait* with the usual 'pa-pa-pah, pa-pa-pah, pa-pa-pah' Pearl & Dean theme music to close out. The curtains drew back again, across in front of the screen. Virtual silence from the audience, only the odd whisper and crackle of popcorn packets. Then the curtains drew back again and projected onto the screen was a much, much larger image of the lady water-skier with JAWS towering out of the water behind her accompanied by the amazing John Williams' *JAWS* musical score. I heard Julia give a little gasp and hoped that this was going to be okay for her. Heidi talked to her softly in German.

The film started. "A few years ago a shark tragedy happened here in Amity…but there is now a new hotel and the promise of a perfect summer…but how could there have been only one? Just when you thought it was safe to get back in the water!" 'Dum-Dum, Dum-Dum'…that wonderful, threatening, almost sickening, huge double-beat from John Williams' orchestration. Action shots of all the main actors, Roy Scheider (police chief), Murray Hamilton (mayor) and Lorraine Gary. The opening scene is of two divers on the ocean floor in full diving gear investigating a wrecked small yacht, then 'Dum-Dum, Dum-Dum', no sight of JAWS yet, but it is clear what is about to happen. A small squeal from Julia as the divers are attacked, killed and then quiet. Serious doubts were now in my mind about how this was going to affect her over the next two hours.

Chief Brody is trying to convince the city council that there is, once again, a shark problem, but they don't want to know. They have all invested heavily in the new hotel. Now for the water-skiing lady…she is being towed fast by her mother in a small speed boat. They're not far out to sea but are on their own. A white-haired old lady is sitting in front of her old house, on her porch, just back from the beach…half dozing, half watching them. The young lady skier is enjoying herself, turning rhythmically, gracefully from side to side, using the speed of the boat to dig her ski into the water and change direction. Then, some way off behind her, the triangular fin appears above the ocean surface, 'Dum-Dum, Dum-Dum'.

"*Vorsicht!!! Oh nien*," whispered Julia, under her breath.

The shark sinks invisibly below the surface and speeds up, getting closer and closer, the camera shot switches back and forth from her smiling face to the speeding shark as it gains on her, seeing the swirling spray trail from her ski, then underneath her water ski and then it strikes, dragging her under. She disappears, the tow line goes slack and all that is left bobbing about on the ocean surface is the empty water ski. Her mother slows and turns the boat around to pick her up, oblivious to the carnage. She slowly motors back, pulling in the tow line and finds the floating empty water-ski. She calls for her daughter, leans over to get to the ski, and as she does, the shark fin rises out of the surface again a way off from the other side of the boat, coming slowly towards her back. 'Dum-Dum, Dum-Dum', then it speeds up, hits the boat hard and takes a big bite out of the side. She is knocked over and turns to see JAWS, mouth wide-open with huge teeth chewing her boat. She screams and picks up a large, heavy jerry-can full of fuel to throw at it, but she wobbles, spills fuel on herself, the boat and the shark's mouth and, finally, drops the can. In desperation, she grabs a flare gun, aims and tries to fire it at the shark's head. It catches fire, so does she and the entire boat. Seconds later, there is a huge explosion and the boat turns in to an inferno, flames towering up into the air. The old lady on her porch jolts awake and sees the blazing boat; wide-eyed and terrified, she rocks in her chair.

"*Mein Got*," said Julia, not so quietly this time. People started to look around at her. Heidi put her arm around her shoulder and shushed her.

The film continued with more pleading from Chief Brody that the beach be closed but no deal. Next is a teenage couple in a small, bright red sailing dinghy, 'Tina's Joy'. They are way out to sea. The boy is standing up looking for their picnic and then the shark fin appears, 'Dum-Dum, Dum-Dum', JAWS hits the underside of the boat and the boy falls overboard. The shark pushes the boat along from underneath like a toy away from the boy in the water. Then all is still and quiet.

"Eddie," calls the girl. "What happened?"

"I don't know," calls back the boy, starting to swim back towards the dinghy.

Then the girl turns and sees the shark fin above the water's surface. 'Dum-Dum, Dum-Dum', it is swimming quickly towards the boat.

"Swim faster, Eddie!" she shrieks, panic across her face. "Shark!!! Swim, SWIM!!!"

Eddie swims faster towards her; the shark is already at the boat and dives underneath. She is screaming at him to go faster.

"*Oh schnell, SCHNELL!*" shouted out Julia.

Heidi grabbed her arm. "Ssshush!"

The shark reaches Eddie, drags him under then pushes him out onto the surface and races him, puppet-like, water spraying out either side of him, into the side of the boat. He looks helplessly up into his girlfriend's eyes, raises one arm and is finally dragged under. The water around the boat turns red. The girl is left in the bottom of the boat, looking down at the water, shaking and softly jibbering to herself, rocking to and fro.

"*Oh Mein Got!*" wailed Julia.

People turned around again, looking aggravated and ssshushing her loudly. Heidi gabbed and cuddled her sister closely, quietly reassuring her in German. "It's only a film, no one is actually hurt."

Sam lent over to me and whispered, "I think we should go before we're asked to!" I let Heidi finish consoling her sister.

"Do you think Julia wants to go?" I whispered to her.

"No, she vill be okay," Heidi assured me.

The film went into a period with no shark attacks, just city council arguments, discussions on and around the beach with parents telling their children not to go far out into the water, brothers arguing about going out in sailing dinghies, Chief Brody calling in a favour from the Coast Guard who promised to send over a helicopter to scan the ocean for sharks. Twenty minutes went by with no brutal shark attacks, but we all knew that it wouldn't last, this was *JAWS 2*!

Two sailing dinghies went out at the same time with two young men in each. Two of them were very confident that all would be okay but only one in the second boat was sure, the other was very nervous, but his brother needed him to crew for him. Inevitably, the shark fin appears again once they are a long way out. 'Dum-Dum, Dum-Dum', lots of tension-filled build-up and then the boats are attacked. This time, Julia screamed out loud, and we all agreed it was time to leave. We left as quickly and quietly as we could. One of the usherettes kindly helped us through the dark with her torch. We came out into the bright lights of the cinema lobby, which was empty. Heidi held Julia's arm with both hands, tears of upset and embarrassment ran down Julia's cheeks, her hand covered her face, then there was full-on sobbing. Sam and I stood helplessly by as Heidi hugged her distraught sister. Intermittent, unintelligible German conversation went on, broken by sobs from Julia. Finally, she calmed down a bit.

"She zinks you vill zink she is a baby," Heidi explained. "She iz zo zorry to spoil zer film for you."

"Oh, Heidi, it doesn't matter," I said, looking over at Julia, her head down and arms clutched protectively around herself. "Julia, it doesn't matter, *es machts nicht, vergiss es*," I said to her, hoping I had got it right. Julia looked up at me, tears still rolling down her face. I couldn't help it; I walked over to her and gave her a hug. Her body jerked with a big sob, and she put her arms around me and squeezed tight. I wasn't expecting that! She held on and I wondered what to do next. I didn't want to upset Heidi, neither did I want to embarrass Julia any further. Fortunately, Julia gradually released me, and Sam stepped in wonderfully, going over and also giving her a friendly, comforting hug. To my surprise, Heidi beamed at us both, recognising the genuine, friendly effort to console her sister and make it all right.

"Zank you," blurted Julia, and we all smiled back at her. "Vot vill Mutti zay?" she worried.

"It depends what we tell her," I replied smiling. "I don't want to make things difficult, but we could say that we all enjoyed the film, even if it was rather scary and leave it at that." Heidi and Julia looked at each other uneasily.

"Let's go to the hotel bar, have a drink and agree what's best," I offered.

So that's what we did. We enjoyed a refreshing drink, and Julia quickly told us that she preferred honesty. I agreed that it was always the best thing, even if not always the easiest.

"If your mum tells me off for taking you to a scary film that has upset you, then I will genuinely apologise and take the blame...and actually, Julia, I do owe you an apology, I thought the film would be okay for you and it wasn't; I'm sorry."

Heidi smiled, leant over and gently punched my arm. Julia smiled, then we all laughed and tried to talk about other things...like the two new machines in 'The Lymes' reception. Sam and I promised to show them how to play 'Dig-Dug' when we got back if the machines weren't occupied.

Heidi then surprised us all by asking, "Are zer sharks in England?"

I looked suspiciously at her; surely, she didn't want to scare her poor sister anymore?

"Well, yes," I answered truthfully, adding quickly, "but they are not dangerous. There are sometimes basking sharks off the coast of England, but they have no teeth. They are 'filter feeders', they only eat tiny plankton even if they can be quite big. Anyway, there are none here at the moment!"

Heidi explained to Julia in German, and she looked relieved. We finished our drinks, went back to the car park and I drove us back to the hotel.

Perhaps fortunately, Mr and Mrs Wortmann were just getting out of their Fiat Mirafiori Estate as we drove into the car park. They waited, looking expectantly towards us as we all got out of the mini. Julia immediately ran to them and flung her arms around her mother. She was in tears again, explaining about what had happened. Mrs Wortmann looked at me admonishingly. Mr Wortmann looked serious to start with and then sighed and smiled.

"Vell, zees zings have to be experienced," he said. "Julia vill learn maybe to vait longer vor ze next one!"

"I'm very sorry that the film upset Julia," I started. "I really thought it would be okay."

Heidi looked anxiously at her parents.

"No, no," replied Mr Wortmann, "not your fault, Paul. Julia vill laugh over it zoon!" We all relaxed a bit and agreed to see each other later, after dinner.

"Well, that could have ended a lot worse," Sam observed once we were back in our room. "I wonder if Julia will go in the sea again this holiday!"

"Hmm, I doubt it," I replied. "She seemed very shaken by the whole thing. We'd better be very careful not to joke about it at all."

Dinner that evening was a quiet affair. Mum and Dad had lazed around the hotel, had a game of Scrabble, read their books and had a few drinks. We told them all about the *JAWS*

2 happenings. Mum sympathised with Julia. "Why would anyone pay to go and see people being attacked by a man-eating shark!" she questioned. "No wonder the poor girl was upset."

After their dinner, the Wortmann family joined us at our table, as if to emphasise that everything was okay. Julia still looked a bit red and puffy around her eyes but seemed pretty cheerful, and whilst Mr and Mrs Wortmann enjoyed coffee and liquors with Mum and Dad, we went to reception to see if we could show Heidi and Julia how to play 'Dig-Dug'.

Luckily, it was the fruit machine that was attracting the attention of the other guests who were already there. Dumpty Senior was pumping coin after coin into the slot in the hope of hitting the £50 Jackpot. The machine was making very appreciative musical noises and flashing its lights happily.

Sam primed 'Dig-Dug' with enough coins for a good long go and set about showing the girls the basics of the game. We stood back and let Heidi take the controls. She did pretty well for a first go and quickly got the hang of when to turn and run, when to attack, how to use the deadly harpoon and foot-pump against the dragons and other monsters. She generously let Julia take over after her second go. Julia was a natural at this game. She scored well and clearly was very pleased with herself. We explained a few of the secrets of how to complete this level and what to do during the next.

There is no doubt that the inventors of these games are wonderfully skilled at addiction! Failing to complete a level when you know what you should have done almost forces you to have another go. Getting onto a new level fills you with determination to master the new features and remember them in order to move ever onwards.

Thirty minutes passed without us thinking. Dumpty Senior had run out of change, pronounced that the machine was 'fixed' and a 'con' and stomped off to the bar to have another drink. Heidi had another go at 'Dig-Dug' and got very frustrated because she couldn't master what Julia had just done and failed to complete level 2. She had two ten pence coins left and went over to the fruit machine.

"Don't waste your money on that, Heidi!" I warned.

She turned, poked her tongue out at me and shook her head, laughing, then turned her attention to the various flashing knobs and buttons and looked intently up at the electronic dials. We laughed and turned back to watch Julia reach level 3 to much whooping and cheering. Sam was explaining carefully what to look out for in level 3 when suddenly there was a loud fanfare from the fruit machine, a celebratory tune was blaring out and all the lights were pulsating brightly at the same time. Coins were cascading noisily into the large metal trough. It went on and on. Heidi was jumping up and down with joy. Clenched fists and arms punching the air.

"Oh my God, she's hit the Jackpot!" blurted out Sam.

We all joined Heidi at the fruit machine; she couldn't talk for excitement. The word 'JACKPOT!' was flashing on and off in huge red letters. Still the coins came. Sam emptied her handbag onto one of the reception seats and we all scooped big handfuls of coins into it. Finally, the machine finished clunking bright silver coins into the trough and the music and flashing lights faded. I went quickly back to our room and retuned with two plastic carrier bags and put one inside the other for strength. We emptied Sam's handbag full and all the other coins into the carrier bag and Heidi proudly took charge of it. It weighed a ton! She looked wide-eyed at me.

"I like zis machine!" She laughed. "You can keep 'Dig-Dug'!"

She hauled the £50 of change in the double strength carrier bag into the bar to show her parents, who were both amazed and delighted. The same couldn't be said of Dumpty Senior who watched sulkily from his bar stool making unsportsman-like comments to his wife that he had been robbed and that the jackpot was really his.

After that excitement, we all retired to our rooms.

"Well, I'm glad that Julia was better than Heidi at 'Dig-Dug'," affirmed Sam. "It will help her confidence and to forget about *JAWS 2*."

"I'm sure that Heidi will be okay with that now she has her £50 jackpot." I laughed. "Poor old Dumpty Senior, I wonder how much he put into that machine only for Heidi to win with her first ten pence!"

Friday

When I woke up on Friday morning, the sun was shining brightly through the gap in the curtains. It was seven thirty and I lay lazily thinking about plans for the day. Suddenly, I realised that this was our last day in Swanage. Last chance to really get to know what Heidi felt for me, if anything other than someone who had been good fun for the holiday. What did I really feel? And what would happen after today anyway? What could happen? Germany isn't that far away but far enough to make a real relationship very difficult. We'd hardly even kissed, but I knew that I felt something very strong for Heidi.

Well, at least the weather was on my side. It was very likely that Heidi and Julia would go down to the beach on a sunny day like this. I got up slowly and quietly. Sam was still fast asleep. I got dressed, I would shave later I thought, and I went out into the garden. The sky was blue, just the odd little white cloud idling by. The light breeze was almost warm. What a day this promised to be. Gulls circled and screeched overhead. I went over to the top of the steps that led down to the beach.

The sea was calm, tiny little waves pushed gently onto the sand. The tide was out and the beach was empty. I stood for a while looking out to sea wondering what opportunity there would be to be alone with Heidi. How could I make that happen without it looking too obvious and without rudely excluding Sam or Julia? A morning on the beach would be great because the German girls were almost sure to be there as would we. It would be fun but not in any way private. Maybe the sea would be cold and Julia would stay with her mum on the beach…but cold water hadn't put her off so far. It was nearly eight o'clock and I'd had no bright ideas so I went back to the room. Sam was just waking up.

"Beautiful morning out there," I said cheerfully.

"Good," mumbled Sam.

"Perfect for spending time on the beach," I continued.

"Hmm," Sam grunted.

"Had a good lie-in?" I joked. "Time to get up, lazy!"

Sam eventually got up. I went back to the garden whilst she got dressed. We agreed to wash and brush our teeth after breakfast. When we got to the restaurant, Mum and Dad were already at our usual table.

"Looks like a lovely day," observed Mum. "Perfect for our last day here."

"Yes," I agreed. "Nice for some time on the beach."

At that moment, the Wortmann family came into the restaurant and went to their usual table. We all waved cheerfully and they waved back.

"I think a lazy day is in order today," said Dad. "Good to round off the week relaxing before the drive back home tomorrow."

"Beach sounds good to me," chimed in Sam. "Last chance to add to my rather poor tan!"

"Well, that's the plan then," concluded Dad, and we enjoyed a relaxed breakfast mostly re-capping the week and laughing about the funny bits, there had been plenty.

Back in our room, I shaved and brushed my teeth.

"So, last day then," started Sam, "what are you going to do about Heidi, my love-struck brother?"

"I don't really know," I confessed. "I'm not sure how she feels. It could just be some holiday fun for her, enjoying the attention, something to tell her college friends when she gets back to Germany."

Sam frowned at me and shook her head. "No, I think it's more than that. Trust me. She likes you, really likes you. I can tell. You pay her lots of attention, you let her know that you like her without embarrassing her, you're sporty, you're older than her but not too much, you have a car and a good job; she's impressed by you. You speak German, and most importantly, you're funny, you make her laugh. Along with everything else that's hard to resist."

"Well, thank you," I said genuinely, "but we've hardly had any time alone to get to know each other properly. We haven't had a real kiss yet, just a cycle ride that nearly ended up with Heidi getting stroppy!"

"Oh, she's a strong-willed young lady for sure!" Sam giggled. "But we've both seen a sensitive, caring side of her too. Remember how she looked after Julia after *JAWS 2*? She felt and appreciated our genuine concern too. I think that inside that pretty head is a caring mind and under that gorgeous figure is a good heart. If you feel strongly for her, you should really do something about it today. If I can help by manipulating a situation so that you can be alone together, then I will."

"Thanks, Sam," I responded gratefully, "I certainly feel strongly for her, and I agree about how you say she is. I just don't know where this could go if she does feel anything for me. Germany is quite a long way away and expensive to get to. She has another year to go at college and I won't be there."

"Take it a step at a time," Sam urged. "Find out today if it's worth working out how to see her again. If not, then so be it, but if she wants to, there will be ways. Your company have offices in Germany and you speak the language."

"Sam, I speak holiday German, enough to order a meal or ask for directions. Not enough to do my job," I objected. "I'm already at evening classes twice a week for my business studies qualifications. I have no time to improve my German."

"You have nearly two hours every day on the train," Sam corrected me. "Read language books, buy a 'Walkman' and listen to German language tapes. There are ways if you really want to."

"Okay, I stand corrected," I conceded. "Let's go down to the beach and enjoy the day. What will be will be…and thanks for your offer of help, I will probably need it!"

We were quickly ready, sun protection cream applied, swimming gear on underneath shorts and T-shirts, towels and camera packed, ball found. By ten thirty, we were on the beach in a good spot. The sun shone ever more brightly and the little white clouds had disappeared. Mum and Dad arrived, and we settled down to read, sun bathe, watch the seagulls, other guests and the yachts and boats out at sea. Half an hour later, Mrs Wortmann, Heidi and Julia arrived on the beach. The girls 'mock marched' up to us and sat down.

"May ve join you?" asked Mrs Wortmann smiling, almost apologetically for her girls' forwardness.

"Yes, of course," welcomed Dad. "Please make yourselves at home!"

Heidi beamed at me and shuffled closer. The ritual of getting towels out of bags, shuffling around on the pebbles to find the least uncomfortable spot, putting on sunglasses, etc. all took a few minutes. Mrs Wortmann had brought a small fold-up chair with her to save the discomfort and sat proudly on it like a monarch on her throne.

"No more stones in zer bones!" she announced, clearly proud of her joke in English.

"Very good!" Mum laughed. "I wish I had one!"

We sat and chatted for a while then Heidi snatched up the ball and looked eagerly at us. "Piggy?" she suggested. Heidi and Julia liked the game and the name, especially as neither Sam nor I could explain why it was called that.

We stood in a triangle with the fourth one in the middle and attempted to throw the ball to each other without the one in the middle guessing where it was going next and intercepting it. Julia was a very athletic 'Piggy' and quickly got the ball. Sam less so. In the end, I deliberately did a rather poor throw so that she could get it and have a rest. She looked thankfully at me and we all sat down for a breather.

"Now ve play 'Holiday-in-zer-middle'," announced Heidi, beaming. "You must try to get zer ball being somezing ve have done zis holiday and ze ozers tell vot it iz!"

I could see that Sam wasn't keen, but I thought it was a genius idea and, to be fair, she joined in well, going first as 'Dumpty-in-the-middle'. She ran around after the ball whilst mimicking Dumpty Senior trying to get his shirt off over his head.

"Dumpty, Dumpty!" Heidi shouted loudly as soon as she got it.

She then went into the centre and did 'Ants-in-the-middle', pretending to be me taking jeans off and whirling them around over her head whilst chasing the ball. Julia was laughing so hard that she could barely speak but managed to splurt out, "Ants!"

To her credit, she did a very good 'JAWS-in-the-middle', opening and closing her outstretched, straight arms widely like the jaws of the shark whilst running to and fro. I got that one first and finished with a 'Skittles-in-the-middle', pretending to bowl a ball down the alley. We were all laughing and making rather a lot of noise and were hot with all of our activity so decided that it was time to cool down in the sea. We ran back to our parents. Mrs Wortmann had been watching and laughed as we arrived.

"Good game?" she enquired.

"*Sehr gut!*" confirmed Heidi.

"Are you coming for a paddle in the sea, Mrs Wortmann?" I asked cheerily. I didn't notice Heidi and Julia stop and look anxious.

"No," she replied sharply, her mood changing instantly.

"Go on," I urged. "It will be nice and refreshing for your feet. You don't have to go in very far."

"NO!" she half shouted in reply. She closed her eyes and shook her head slowly.

There was a very awkward silence. Mum and Dad looked at me, almost for guidance. I opened my eyes wide and shrugged. Heidi grabbed my arm and pulled me, running towards the sea. Julia did the same with Sam. We half ran, half stumbled over the pebbles and continued straight into the cold sea.

"She von't go in vorter," gasped Heidi seriously. "Her bruzer died in ze sea ven he vos eight. She vos zer too and just lived."

She continued and told us that when she was ten her mother had been on holiday with her parents and brother in Portugal, the Pacific Algave Coast. There had been some very strong winds and the waves were huge. She and her brother had been playing waist deep in the sea and hadn't seen huge waves behind them. The first crashed onto them knocking her brother unconscious as he hit his head on the sea floor. He then got sucked back out to sea by the undercurrent. She was also knocked flat and had to struggle to get up but just about made it when another huge wave battered her down again. Her parents hadn't seen it happen, but some men playing ball on the beach had and they raced to haul her up out of the immensely strong back swell. They had not been able to find her brother until it was too late. It had taken Heidi's dad a long time to persuade her mum to let the girls learn to swim and then to be allowed to go into the sea. They were never allowed in when it was windy and the waves were big.

I felt terrible. All of the fun of the 'Piggy' game had gone.

"I'm so sorry, Heidi," I said, almost ashamed. "Your poor Mum." I looked back up the beach. Mrs Wortmann was in serious discussion with my parents, clearly explaining the reason for her outburst. They all looked upset and awkward. I knew it wasn't my fault but didn't know how to break the blanket of gloom that had so quickly covered us.

"We need to give them a little time before we go back up," said Sam sensibly, and she started to swim in the shallow water.

"How old ver you ven you learn to svim?" asked Heidi.

"Probably about seven I think," I replied. "We had an open-air swimming pool near where we live and I spent almost every day there in the summer holidays. We also went once a week with the school. It is seen as important to be able to swim in England."

"In Germany also," confirmed Heidi, "but it vos hard vor my mum to allow it."

We soon got cold and decided to go back up the beach. Mrs Wortmann had already gone back up to the garden when we arrived. Mum and Dad looked rather embarrassed as they told Heidi and Julia. They nodded, understanding. We all lay down to absorb the warmth of the sun and hoped that the mood would also warm and change.

Around midday, Mr Wortmann came down to the beach to find his girls. He was his usual friendly self which relaxed us all a bit. His wide smile and kind eyes were a great help and he eagerly told us about his long walk and excellent photos of insects, plants, sky and sea. He made no mention of what had happened, invited Heidi and Julia to go up for lunch and wished us a good afternoon.

I watched as they made their way slowly up the steep steps, looked at Sam and then sighed, lowering my head and shutting my eyes, exhaling loudly.

"It's not your fault, Paul," reassured Mum. "Sylvia said so herself before she went back up. It just takes her by surprise sometimes. She thinks she has banished the memory somewhere deep in her mind when a suggestion like she should go and stand in the sea brings it right back as if it's just happened. She'll be fine once Kurt and the girls spend some time with her and get her thinking about happier things."

But I want Heidi with me this afternoon, I shouted in my head. "*We go home tomorrow morning*!" We decided to wait thirty minutes before going up for lunch. I didn't feel like eating anyway. The Wortmanns were not in the restaurant when we got there.

"Maybe they took a picnic and have gone out for the afternoon," suggested Mum.

"Quite likely on such a lovely day and after..." Dad hesitated. "Well, you know," he finished.

Sam wanted to carry on topping up her suntan on the beach. Mum and Dad wanted to go for a gentle walk and then relax and read. I decided to go for another cycle ride and after lunch went to find Alec to open the garden shed for me. I found him, as usual, behind the bar.

"May I borrow a bike this afternoon please, Alec?" I asked. "Just the one this time."

He raised his eyebrows and looked at me quizzically, expecting me to explain why the 'pretty wee lassie' wasn't coming with me this time.

"On your own then?" he asked.

"'Fraid so, Alec. Heidi has gone out with her family and Sam wants to sunbathe," I explained.

"Okay then, give me ten minutes," he agreed.

We walked around to the shed together.

"Shame she's not going with you," said Alec, "I've noticed a kind of" – he hesitated – "Well, a kind of 'clicking' between the two of you, kindred spirits shall we say, nice to see."

"Yes, I know," I agreed. "It's a real shame because it's my last afternoon. I go home tomorrow morning."

"She's here all next week, you know," advised Alec quickly, not wanting to change the subject.

"Yes, that's right. I know, thanks," I confirmed. "I'm back to work in London on Monday so couldn't get back even if—"

"Oh…oh, well…no…I see," interrupted Alec, stumbling through his sentence sensing, incorrectly, that I didn't want to talk about things.

I liked Alec. He seemed to care about people in a way that most of 'The Lymes' staff did not. Despite seeming to be a bit of a 'loner', he observed carefully, insightfully and seemed to understand about people and relationships.

"Alec, no secrets," I started, "I had hoped to spend this afternoon finding out if Heidi feels anything for me that's worth developing, you know, growing, even though she lives in Germany, but it looks like that won't happen."

"Hmm, difficult," mused Alec. "There's always this evening," he encouraged. "If I can help, just tip me the wink." He smiled kindly at me as we reached the shed.

I selected the same white bike as I'd used on Wednesday and set off, following the same route as before. I enjoyed the ride. There was virtually no traffic despite it being a sunny Friday afternoon. I remembered our Wednesday ride as I went past the same places. I stopped to get a drink at the same village store in Acton. I cycled slowly past the vantage point in Worth Matravers where we had stopped to look out to sea and I had complemented her on her pretty face and great figure. That quick kiss on the lips shot back into my mind. I stopped in Woolgarston and pushed the bike into the field where we had lain down and held hands. I sat down and closed my eyes. I felt how her hand had gripped mine. I remembered the playful, no, more than playful, punch on the arm. Heidi hadn't wanted to go back to the hotel. She had wanted to stay here, in this field, holding my hand. What would have happened if I had let us stay and risked being in trouble for being back late? Why had I not taken advantage of the fact that Heidi had wanted to stay here with me? She was annoyed that I wanted us to go back. Was she annoyed because she thought I didn't want to stay and hold hands, maybe kiss her properly? Was she annoyed because she felt spurned or because she wanted to be in charge and I wouldn't let her?

Whatever the reason, I hadn't made the most of a really great opportunity to ask her how she felt. At least, I had made it clear that I really liked her and she had, after all, kissed me on the lips, albeit quickly and giving me no chance to immediately respond…but I hadn't kissed her back, here in this field when I had the ideal opportunity…IDIOT!

I got up, got back on the bike and cycled slowly back to 'The Lymes' all the while chastising myself mentally for being so stupid, so responsible for the current situation I was in.

It was half past four when I got back. I checked the car park for the Wortmanns' Mirafiori, but it wasn't there. I put the bike carefully behind the shed and went to reception to let them know so that Alec could lock up later. I went slowly through the garden, no Mum and Dad. Then slowly, I went down to the beach and found Sam, half asleep in the sun. She heard me as I crunched over the pebbles towards her.

"Don't get sunburnt!" I warned gently, feeling a bit lost, having no idea what I wanted to do next.

"Hmm," responded Sam lazily. "Maybe time to stop. I do feel rather well done! How was the bike ride?"

"Well, it made me think that I should have been bolder, not my cycling, but when I had the chance on my own with Heidi."

"Oh, what happened?" she asked, sitting up.

I sighed. "I kind of told you, we sat down in a field for a while and Heidi wanted to stay but I insisted that we should go to make sure that we got back at the time I had promised her parents. I could easily have spent another fifteen minutes with her with no one else around. I should have done that. We could have said a lot to each other in those fifteen minutes."

"Hence her bad mood when you got back," remembered Sam.

"Yes, as we said she is used to getting her own way! Anyway, the ride gave me some exercise and time to think and it killed a couple of hours. What's next?" I enquired.

"Shower and more rest!" advised Sam. "Mum and Dad went for a walk, and I said we'd meet up at six thirty for last night drinks and dinner!"

Which we did. In fact, we joined Mum and Dad and the Wortmann family for drinks in the bar before dinner. Nothing more was said about what happened on the beach and Mrs Wortmann was her usual lovely self again. Dad and Mr Wortmann were talking about cars. Kurt was explaining why he had an Italian car when the Germans were so renowned for their excellent vehicles.

"It is gut to be different," he said. "It is orange and zer are not many Mirafioris in Frankfurt. It has a quick acceleration even if not a huge engine and I can afford it!"

"I'm very lucky that the bank provide mine for me," said Dad. "I wouldn't want to pay for the lovely Vauxhall that I have, nor for the fuel or insurance…but it is not very 'different'! I'm glad you can afford to be different in Frankfurt, Kurt!"

"How much does a car cost?" asked Heidi.

"Anything from a few hundred pounds to many thousands!" advised Dad. "There is a big second-hand car market in the UK. Not many people want to pay for a brand-new one."

"Zis is rare in Germany," observed Mr Wortmann. "Most people buy a new car zat zey can afford and keep it a long time."

"I can't imagine ever having enough money to buy a new car!" I stated. "Not *and* be able to afford to pay rent or a mortgage!"

"Best not to worry about that now," Dad responded. "You're doing well, Paul; your little mini is perfect for you right now."

"I like it!" chipped in Heidi. "To have a mini in Frankfurt vood be different!"

Mum and the rest of the ladies were in deep conversation about something else and it took a prompt from Alec for us to go to our tables and order dinner when Dad went to the bar for another round.

The Wortmanns went to their favourite table. We wished them a good meal and took our drinks with us, sat down and selected our favourite dishes for the last time.

We finished dinner and were now at a loss to find something to do. How to get Heidi on her own was my priority. Take her for a walk in the garden or down to the beach maybe? What if she said no? After all, it was windy and it looked like it might rain. What if she said yes, but Sam and Julia decided that they wanted to come along too? Sam had said that she would help to create a good situation for me, but it was too risky. It had to be something that would really work, nothing left to chance.

We left our parents at the table, met up with Heidi and Julia again and sat down in the lounge area by the bar. It was quite busy and our quietness contrasted starkly with the babble and chatter of the post-dinner drinkers around the bar. Julia was looking around for her mum and dad. Heidi was sitting on the chair beside her, strangely quiet. I wondered what she was thinking about and nearly asked her but then thought better of it.

"Our parents are making that second coffee last!" said Sam, breaking the silence.

"Dad will be having another brandy if I know him!" I laughed.

"Maybe we can play cards," suggested Sam. "Would you like a game, girls?"

"Okay." Heidi shrugged. "Vot game can ve play?"

"Snap!" jumped in Julia.

"Oh no," said Heidi and I together and then we both laughed.

"Whist is a good game for four players," I offered.

"Visk?" queried Heidi; Julia giggled.

"No, WHIST!" I emphasised. "It's a game where you play to win hands by keeping to the suit that is played or by using whichever suit is trumps." I was about to continue when I realised from the looks that Heidi and Julia were giving me that I may as well have been talking Chinese!

"I think that it will be easiest to demonstrate with the cards," I said. "Shall I go and get them?"

"Okay." Heidi shrugged again.

"I'll go," offered Sam, "I need to use the loo anyway."

Damn! I had hoped that Heidi might offer to come to the room with me to find the cards, an opportunity missed.

Sam went to get the pack of playing cards. Whilst she was gone, I had another go at explaining to the girls the rules of Whist.

"The cards are all dealt out equally to the four players so that each player has thirteen. Each player then sorts their cards into suits, you know, Clubs, Hearts, Diamonds and Spades," I began.

"Diamonds are trumps for the first hand followed by the other suits in turn with Spades last," I continued, looking at both girls to see if they had understood so far. Julia nodded, but Heidi looked disinterested.

I persevered. "The player to the left of the dealer—"

"Mutti!" called Heidi and waved to her mother who had just walked into the lounge area with Kurt and my parents.

All four of them came over to our table and group of seats.

"Vot vill you do now?" asked Mr Wortmann, smiling broadly at us all. Mrs Wortmann smiled too and looked a little pink in the face from the good dinner and generous helpings of alcohol.

"Paul vill show us his Visk!" blurted Heidi, laughing out loud; Julia sniggered loudly too.

"Sam has gone to fetch the playing cards and we may be going to play 'Whist' if I can help Heidi and Julia understand how to play," I corrected them, giving Heidi a mock sideways glance.

"*Gut gluck!*" replied Mr Wortmann laughing. "But zey vill cheat!"

"I don't think you can cheat at whist!" I replied.

"You vill see." Mr Wortmann laughed, winking at Heidi. "Ve vill go for a vork in ze garten until it rains," he finished and offered his arm to his wife, who did a mock courtesy, giggled and took his arm, squeezing it tightly to her.

"That's a good idea," joined in Dad, following Kurt's lead and offering Mum his arm. All four walked off towards the garden. Mrs Wortmann turned and waved at the last minute, giving us all a cheeky look that clearly meant she was enjoying herself very much.

"She vill sleep vell tonight!" observed Heidi smiling, but then she puffed her cheeks out in boredom, and I was worried that she might join her parents in the garden. Luckily, Sam

101

retuned at that moment with the cards. I did my best 'professional' shuffling of the pack and then dealt the cards into four equal piles. We spent ten more minutes demonstrating how to play with the hands of cards turned face up. Heidi and Julia caught on quickly. It seemed they, not surprisingly, played a very similar game in Germany. We were soon playing for real. The first hand ended and I realised that we needed to keep score.

"I'll go and get some paper and a pencil," I offered, "we don't want you mistakenly thinking that you've won, do we?" I added, winking at Heidi. She hesitated and then, arriving at a full understanding of what I had said, blew a large raspberry at me and looked indignant, but then her face changed and she opened her eyes wider.

"I come too," she said unexpectedly, almost excitedly. "You must have my address to zend presents!"

"Er, okay," I fumbled, "I s'pose we could write to each other."

"Presents!" insisted Heidi, smirking and getting up out of her chair.

We walked together towards the lounge door, and I wondered what I was going to do now that I had the opportunity to be alone with Heidi, very much at her bidding. Suddenly, I realised that Sam had the door key so I quickly ran back, plucked the key from the tabletop and re-joined Heidi. As I reached her, her eyes fixed mine. They blazed bright blue straight through to my brain. My heart pounded. I hoped that I wasn't misreading that gaze…but I couldn't be. We went along the narrow corridor in single file, me leading and seemed to reach the room very quickly. I opened the door, switched on the light and went over to the dressing table to get the pencil and paper. I heard the door click shut and turned to find myself staring straight into those incredible blue eyes again. Wide open, almost as if they were scared but somehow drawing me across the room into them. On auto-pilot, I made it across the room, holding her gaze, and suddenly, we were kissing. A deep passionate kiss, frantically releasing the pent-up longing of the last five days. Holding each other, her arms behind my shoulders pulling me onto her, my hands on her waist. She was pressed back against the door and I could feel the firm push of her breasts against my chest. She moved her hands and pulled my head closer into hers and kissed even deeper. Eventually, we had to separate. I stepped back a bit. Heidi beamed at me, her fair complexion flushed red, her beautiful blue eyes sparkling. I put my left hand out and gently stroked her curly blonde hair back from her face. She took my hand, pulled it to her mouth and gently bit my finger and laughed. I laughed too and then we kissed again, more slowly this time but still passionate, long and gentle, mouths and tongues entwined. We stopped the kiss and hugged for what seemed ages.

"We'd better go back soon," I said reluctantly. "They'll be wondering where we are!"

"Okay," agreed Heidi dreamily, still beaming from ear to ear, "but you still need my address!"

I got the things from the dresser and we left the room. I locked the door and started to walk slowly along the narrow corridor. Heidi pushed next to me and took my hand. I squeezed it strongly and we smiled, looking wide-eyed at each other. We walked slowly back to the lounge. Just as we reached the lounge, Heidi let go of my hand and looked at me apologetically. I nodded; this was something to keep to ourselves for the moment. We awkwardly re-joined Sam and Julia, who by then had got and consumed half a drink.

"Here's the scoring equipment," I said, putting the pencil and paper on the table as casually as I could. Sam looked at me knowingly and opened her eyes wide looking for a response. I simply smiled back and nodded.

"Coke for you, Heidi?" I asked matter-of-factly.

"*Danke*," she replied, still beaming.

"*Bitte*," I said happily, turning and walking over to the bar as if I had springs in my soles. I queued for what seemed like a very long time, but eventually, Alec got free and served me. He looked at my face and seemed to know instantly.

"Well," he said cheerfully, "something celebratory this evening, Paul!" And he winked in the direction of our table where Heidi had just sat down and was looking intently towards me.

"Just the usual please, Alec and a coke for the lady!" And I winked back.

"Certainly!" He looked genuinely cheered up, lifted by my happiness. He breezed about the bar getting our drinks as if he owned the whole hotel!

I eventually returned to the table with the drinks, by which time Sam and Julia had finished theirs and wanted refills requiring me to make a return visit to the bar. Alec was straight over this time, ignoring another couple who were really first in the queue.

"I'll be with you in just a tick," he said to them and looked me straight in the eye again.

"I haven't seen a face as bright and cheerful as yours right now for a very long time, well done!!!" he whispered and got a repeat round for Sam and Julia without me having to specify their drinks.

"Thanks, Alec." I beamed, absorbing his good wishes gratefully and feeling like I'd never felt before. I didn't care if everyone in the room knew! I was in love and had just kissed the most beautiful girl on earth.

By the time I got back to the girls, the parental group had come back in from the garden and were pulling up chairs to the table.

"Not playing cards then?" observed Dad.

"Not yet!" replied Sam pointedly.

"Probably a bit late now," I suggested, looking at my watch which said ten fifteen.

"Well, we all need to pack our things tonight," said Mum. "We want to get a prompt start after breakfast tomorrow."

Suddenly, it hit me. We were leaving tomorrow morning straight after breakfast. Virtually, no more chance to be with Heidi alone. I downed the rest of my beer and said boldly, "I'm going for a last bit of sea air before packing."

"I need air," chipped in Heidi quickly.

Knowing looks passed between Sam and Julia and then Julia and Mrs Wortmann.

"I'll start my packing," said Sam by way of diversion, smiling warmly at me. "May I have the key, please?"

Heidi and I walked into the garden together, close but not holding hands. Then down the steep steps to the beach. We walked, kissed, hugged and walked some more. By the time we got back to the steps, it was eleven o'clock.

"I vill get up early tomorrow," Heidi murmured leaning against me.

"*Gut*," I murmured back. "*Sieben uhr.*"

"*Sieben uhr?*" blurted back Heidi.

"*Sieben uhr,*" I confirmed, "*Sieben hier, an der strand,*" I insisted. "*Sieben uhr? ... Sieben uhr!*" She sighed.

"Okay!"

One last good-night kiss and we went back up the steps, over to the lounge where we separated and went dreamily off to our rooms.

Sam had left the door on the latch and was asleep in the dark. I set my alarm, undressed and got into bed. I closed my eyes and enjoyed at least another hour of a warm, satisfied yet very excited feeling.

Saturday – Home – Sunbury-on-Thames

Six thirty AM came around very quickly. I threw as much as I could, as quietly as I could, into my suitcase, got dressed, brushed my teeth, combed my hair and very quietly left our room. Breakfast started at seven thirty and the sounds of the busy kitchen filled the corridor. Pots and saucepans bashed, crockery clattered and cutlery chinked as I went quickly through the lounge and out into the garden. It was a bright but not very sunny morning, with a fresh breeze. I was a bit early and I knew that Heidi wouldn't be there yet, but still, I made my way slowly down the steps to the beach. I startled a small flock of gulls as I reached the pebbles, and they flew seawards, squawking loudly their disapproval.

"It's only me," I said to them, for some stupid reason.

The empty beach looked lovely in the early morning light. The waves pushed the pebbles around in the usual way and the clouds sped across the sky majestically. I walked slowly around to the right, put my hands in my pockets to keep them warm and waited. There was no doubt that Heidi would arrive, the only thing in question was when. I stood with my eyes closed, listening to the rhythmic, soothing sound of the sea. Then I heard the crunch of pebbles and there was Heidi, yellow-blonde curly hair a bit ruffled from sleep, in tight blue jeans, white sweatshirt and trainers. She came close and we kissed. I could smell the clean, 'just washed' smell of her face over the slightly dirty, salty smell of the beach.

"I could come back next Saturday and see you," I whispered. "I'm sure I can find a little hotel to stay in."

Heidi did a quiet kind of squeal. "Yes," she whispered. "Bevor I go home."

We walked slowly along the beach, arms around each other, talking by touch. We sat on the dry pebbles smiling into each other's eyes, unable to articulate much but feeling entirely comfortable and exhilarated. Time seemed to stand still…but it didn't. Too soon, it was eight o'clock.

"You vill come, von't you?" urged Heidi, looking at me a bit anxiously.

"Nothing will stop me," I promised, meaning every word and kissed her.

We went reluctantly back up for breakfast. I promised to phone and leave a message with 'The Lymes' reception ladies for Heidi confirming where I would stay and when I would meet her at the same spot on the beach next Saturday morning. As we made our way to the restaurant, we exchanged one last, long look and then joined our respective families.

"Ah, Paul, there you are," said Mum. "We've ordered you cereal, toast and tea."

"Thanks, perfect," I said cheerfully and turned to Sam. "All packed? Everything okay?"

"Yes, thanks," she replied. "Sorry I was asleep when you got back last night. Have you packed your stuff?"

"Pretty much," I lied. "I won't take long with breakfast and I'll be done in no time."

"I thought you'd be all packed by now," said Dad tetchily. "We want to make a quick getaway once we're done here."

"Don't worry, Dad, Sam and I will catch you up if we're not ready when you want to set off." I laughed. Sam winked at me and I thanked her with a smile.

Breakfast over, I hurried back to the room, finished packing and took our cases to reception. Dad was there settling the bill.

"Thanks for a great week, Dad," I said.

"Yeah, Paul had a great time!" teased Sam.

"I think we all have," countered Mum.

"Yes, but Paul had a really GREAT time," persisted Sam.

"All right, all right, you'll be carrying your own suitcase to the car if you're not careful!" I retaliated.

The manager of the hotel arrived at that point and thanked us all for spending the week at 'The Lymes' and wished us a safe journey home. I carried our luggage through the car park and loaded it into the boot of the mini. No sign of the Wortmanns, but I hadn't expected that. Heidi seemed to want to be quite secretive about it all, but what about next weekend? Everyone would have to know by then!

I opened the passenger door for Sam, got into the driver's seat and fired the mini up. She started wonderfully easily, a good omen for the journey home.

The roads were busy as expected but no dramatic hold ups or overheating, and we were home in two and a half hours. Home seemed like somewhere entirely different for the first three hours or so – no seaside noises or garden, no steep steps, no pebble beach, no gulls…and no Heidi. We all got into the routine of unpacking, putting things for washing in one pile and carefully putting away the still clean things that we hadn't needed anyway! Mum made a late lunch and I selected some music to listen to. I put on Nat King Cole, Mum's favourite, and the first track was *Unforgettable*. I stared out of the window onto the front garden, and as the music and lyrics penetrated my brain, my stomach developed a painful, yawning, great empty hole that no food was going to fill. Suddenly, the music stopped. Sam was laying the table and had obviously seen me staring out of the window and had lifted the play arm away from the record.

"Not the best choice I think," she said gently.

I turned and faced her. "You're right," I agreed, my throat thick with emotion. "You choose something."

"Oh, Paul, what are you going to do about this?" she asked, concerned. "I'll go back down next weekend and see her," I confirmed.

"Yes, but after that," she continued, "how will you manage?"

"I don't know," I replied truthfully, "I really don't know."

We had a quiet meal passing complementary memories of the holiday. When we reached the dessert stage, I mentioned that I might go back down to Swanage the following weekend to see Heidi and her family. No one was surprised. Dad graciously offered to help find a hotel for the Saturday night, well, he offered to get his secretary to do it!

Monday – Back at Work

Back at work on Monday, I had all the usual questions from colleagues about the holiday. Several of the more bawdy men asked about any good-looking girls but I kept things safely to myself. In the afternoon I got a call from Dad.

"Hello Paul, we've found a small hotel with a single room, bed and breakfast close to the beach. It's called The Grafton Hotel."

"Brilliant, thanks, Dad," I said very gratefully.

The week dragged by badly. I was busy with a week's worth of work to catch up on but found it difficult to concentrate for thinking about seeing Heidi again and desperately trying to think of the right gift to take her. In the end I decided to look for a small, silver St Christopher pendant and chain. I couldn't find what I wanted so decided to clean up the one that I usually wore and give her that plus the current 'Commodores' hit single *Three Times a Lady*.

Saturday – The Grafton Hotel – Swanage

I packed a few things on Friday night, called 'The Lymes' and spoke to Alec. I asked him to make sure that Heidi got a note or that he spoke to her personally to tell her that I would be waiting for her on the beach by the hotel at nine thirty Saturday morning. He took the responsibility very seriously and agreed without hesitation. I set off at 6.00 am on Saturday morning to be sure to miss the traffic. I took my faithful battery-powered Philips tape machine and my 'Santana' tapes. The journey was really easy with virtually nothing on the roads, and as I reached to top of Hartland Moor Hill and looked down at Swanage beach with the sea sparkling in the early morning sun, my favourite track started with a magical melody and Carlos Santana playing the guitar soulfully, as only he can, it all seemed unreal, like watching a film, but I knew that I would see Heidi soon.

I got to Swanage and, after a bit of a drive around, I found Gilbert Road and the rather old-fashioned looking 'Grafton Hotel'. I parked on the road outside and realised that I was desperate for a wee! It was seven forty-five. I locked the car and walked up the short path, opened the glass-paned front door and went into the hotel reception. There was no one behind the reception desk. In fact, there was no sign of anyone anywhere, but I saw a sign with an arrow to 'The Conveniences'. Confident that no one would mind me using them since I had booked a room, I followed the arrows down various corridors and down one flight of stairs finally, and very thankfully finding the Gents. Having relieved myself and washed my hands, I followed the arrows back, in reverse, to reception. A short, dark-haired man of around fifty was now behind the desk studying some papers intently. He was wearing a brightly coloured, paisley pattern waistcoat and matching bow-tie and, from what I could see with his head slightly down, he had a small 'Hitler-style' moustache.

I stopped close to the reception desk, my soft-soled shoes made virtually no sound and he clearly hadn't heard me. I waited quietly, expecting him to look up, but he was miles away in his papers, humming contentedly to himself. I looked around the reception area taking in the cheesy, cheap, chintzy

111

interior decoration and curtains. Hung on many of the walls were framed old and more recent flyers for 'The Swanage Drama Company' who had obviously put on several Pantos, including *Dick Whittington* and *Jack and the Beanstalk*, some comedies including *Funny Man* and a version of *Carry On Doctor* that they had named *Carry On Matron* There were also some more serious efforts with a big poster for *And Then There Were None*. From the black and white photos of the star characters in the plays, I gathered that the man that I was about to speak to was a regular 'player'.

He suddenly realised that he wasn't alone, looked up at me and jumped, stepping back slightly. He put down the papers that were in his hand and looked at me challengingly.

"I didn't hear you come through the front door," he said loudly in a rather tense and very camp voice.

"I came back up from The Conveniences!" I advised, smiling. "There was no one in reception when I came in through the front door."

We stood staring at each other a moment, his face a picture of disapproval.

"Well, you should have waited," he flustered. "We can't have uninvited people wandering all over the hotel. We don't do that at 'The Grafton'!" He shook his head dramatically as he finished; his upper torso shook with his head.

"I was desperate," I explained calmly, "I have just driven almost two hours to get here…and I'm not uninvited, I have booked a room for tonight."

He looked a little less aggressive. "And you are?"

"Paul Gardener," I confirmed.

He pulled a large, black battered hard-backed book across the counter towards himself and opened it theatrically, dabbing his finger on his tongue each time he turned a page like it was some precious antique document. I was quite enjoying the encounter; he was entertaining, if a bit painful! He found the relevant page and ran his finger slowly down the left-hand column, glancing up at me as he did it. His finger stopped, he pointed and then struck an entry firmly, triumphantly.

"Mr Gardener. One night only. Bed and breakfast," he read out dramatically and looked up enquiringly at me.

"That's it," I agreed, "I'm just staying tonight and having breakfast here tomorrow morning."

"I see. Good." He hesitated. "Gordon Grafton…My hotel," he concluded seriously and held out his hand. I shook it in a friendly way.

"Paul Gardener, your guest!" I went back cheekily. He laughed out loud, genuinely enjoying the retort.

"Excellent! You'll be wanting to book in for dinner tonight as well?" he ventured.

"No, thank you," I replied, "I'm meeting with friends this evening."

"Hmm, shame," he said, "Chef has some lovely steaks for this evening. We can't tempt you?"

"Sorry, no," I said, reasonably firmly to leave no doubt. "Arrangements have already been made." And as I said this, I wondered what I was going to do for a meal that evening!

"Well, shame, but okay…Room 2," he confirmed, smiled, span theatrically on the ball of his right foot and went over to a closed cabinet on the back wall. He took a small key out of his waistcoat pocket and opened the cabinet. He pulled the key for Room 2 from its hook and minced back to the counter where he put it firmly down, the cheap plastic fob bouncing up.

"I'll just go and get my case from the car," I said. "I parked on the road in front of your hotel. Is there a car park I may leave it in please?"

"Certainly," he boasted, "drive down Gilbert Road for twenty yards, turn left and then left again at the sign for 'The Grafton Hotel car park'." He gestured flamboyantly, waving his hand in the direction of the front door. "We don't advertise it out front. You never know who may want to just plonk their vehicle in it!" he said.

"Thanks. I'll be back in a few minutes for the key."

"I'll be here waiting," he said, smiling again. "We don't want you roaming all over the hotel again, do we!" And he fluttered his eyelids.

I followed his directions, parked the car, came back into the hotel through the back door and followed the signs for reception. G. Grafton esquire was still behind the counter and graciously gave me my key and directions to the room.

Room 2 was a tiny, barely decorated single room with a bed and a very small wardrobe. The bathroom and toilet were two doors down the corridor. I unpacked, tested the bed for comfort and went to the bathroom for a shave. Having done that, I consulted the street map of Swanage that Dad had somehow got for me. All I needed to do was head straight for the seafront and follow it until I found 'The Lymes'. It was only eight thirty so I had a good thirty minutes before I needed to set off. I lay on the bed thinking about seeing Heidi again, not just seeing her but holding and kissing like we had done a week ago. I had a warm inner glow, not nerves but excitement, expectation. There had been few moments that week when

Heidi hadn't pushed her way into my mind and it was now only about an hour or so before I could look into those fabulous blue eyes again and feel her strong body holding me tight. I checked the small bag that contained her presents. The 'Commodores' record and small jewellery box with my sparkly clean St Christopher inside were there. I was sure that she would like them. Something to keep close to her when she was back in Germany. It would be months before we could be together again. I had checked the holiday rota at work and I couldn't have any time off until the end of October. I had provisionally booked a week off and would check with Heidi if that worked for her. I hoped it might be half-term time in Germany. I wondered what her parents' apartment was like in Frankfurt. I was used to the luxury of a big four-bedroomed house with large gardens front and back. I'd never thought about what it would be like for a family of four to live in an apartment in a block of flats in a big city. My mind wandered as I lay with my eyes closed. I came too and checked my watch. It was five to nine. Time to go.

I left my key at reception with the flamboyant Mr Grafton and set off. It was a much easier journey than I had imagined and I found 'The Lymes' within fifteen minutes. I parked the mini in the car park near to the Wortmanns' Mirafiori Estate. I got out, stretched and walked slowly into the garden and across to the top of the steps down to the beach. It was a glorious morning and there were a few guests looking around the garden. I didn't recognise any of them, they had probably arrived the same weekend we left.

I waited by the top of the steps for a while but felt rather conspicuous so descended to the beach and waited there instead. I had mentally prepared for Heidi to be at least fifteen minutes late so when it reached nine forty-five, I wasn't unduly worried. I sat down on the pebbles and occupied myself by looking for interesting stones. Looking carefully at them, the variety of colours and textures were amazing. From very black and shiny to orangey-brown with pits and pores all over them.

Particles of shells were everywhere. There were a good number of white chalky pebbles with their flint 'cousins' nearby. Even with an interest in geology, there is only so much time during which the inspection of pebbles on a beach is absorbing, especially when you're waiting for a beautiful girl!

It was nearly ten o'clock, and I was getting just a little concerned when I heard the crunch of pebbles and quick steps coming towards me. I stood up and turned around and there was Heidi hurrying towards me. She flung herself into my arms.

"Paul, Paul!" she shouted hoarsely in my ear. "I vaited by zer steps, but you didn't come!"

"I said that I would be on the beach! Didn't you see my car in the car park?" I replied pushing her gently back so that I could look into her eyes. They were wide with concern and excitement. She smiled at me and punched my arm.

"Silly," she said, "you make me vorry!"

I pulled her to me and kissed her gently on the lips several times. She responded but clearly wanted a deeper, more passionate kiss. We held each other tightly and gradually both calmed down. We walked, arms around each other slowly along the beach.

"I have a very small room in a funny hotel with a very strange owner!" I laughed and told her about my encounter with Gordon Grafton.

"I vont to meet him." Heidi giggled. "He zownds very funny."

"I'm sure that I can arrange that," I joked back. "I will show you just how different hotels can be in Swanage!"

We walked arm-in-arm, chatting about our separate weeks for what seemed ages. We turned and walked back along the beach, this time planning the day and a half that we would have together.

"My farzer vonts us all to go vork along zer clifftop to zee nature!" Heidi moaned.

"I'd really like that," I said positively. "It's a wonderful walk and a beautiful day."

"But I vont to be viz you," she protested.

"You will be with me," I reassured her.

She looked down and then slowly up, holding her head at 'half-mast'. Her big beseeching eyes telling me that is not what she meant by 'being with me'.

"I know, I know," I said and held her close, "but let's not upset your dad the moment I get here. We'll have a chance to be alone when I show off the 'Grafton Hotel' later on!"

She nodded into my chest and stayed there. I moved back slightly and gently lifted her chin with my right hand. I gazed meaningfully into her beautiful eyes, silently telling her that I knew exactly what she meant and kissed her gently.

"We'll find a way to spend some private time together without upsetting your parents," I whispered. "Trust me."

She nodded slowly and agreed that we should go back up to the garden and meet her family. She led the way up the steps and we walked side-by-side but not holding hands, to the Wortmann family who were sat at a table enjoying the late morning sunshine. They all stood up, and I shook hands with Mr and Mrs Wortmann. Julia smiled welcomingly, and they asked me about my journey down and then we discussed the walking route.

Mr Wortmann had it all carefully planned and no one argued! It felt surprisingly natural to be out walking with this German family even though I had only known them for a week. If the circumstance seemed in any way strange to them, they didn't show it. From time to time, Heidi and Julia ran off together, down a grassy bank to hide or up a steep hillock to march theatrically along the top – just playing like close sisters do. Mr and Mrs Wortmann took these opportunities to, very politely, find out as much as they could about me and what, if anything, I planned with regard to their Heidi once their holiday finished and they had returned to Germany.

"Well, I will write to her and hope that she will write back," I said earnestly, looking straight at Mrs Wortmann, "and if she would like, I can come over to Frankfurt at the end of October to see her again, but I haven't talked to her about that yet."

"Oh, she vill write back, I know it," Mrs Wortmann replied, smiling and nodding. She held her husband's arm by the elbow. "She likes you."

"And I like her very much. I wouldn't do anything to hurt her," I reassured them both.

"Ve zink you are a nice boy viz a good family," said Mr Wortmann, his turn to talk earnestly. "Our Heidi iz still young even if she zinks not!"

Heidi and Julia returned breathlessly, cutting short that conversation.

"*Ich habe hunger!*" announced Julia.

Her father playfully held the large picnic bag protectively to his side, away from her.

"*Noch nicht, lieblings* (Not yet, darlings)," he said, in mock seriousness.

Both girls fell to the floor as if on their last legs. "*Bitte, Papa*!!!" they pleaded, arms outstretched, the palms of their hands open and slightly raised up. Mrs Wortmann and I laughed. He gave in straight away, and we found a good spot with a great view and enjoyed 'The Lymes' best picnic lunch together. Once again, I was surprised at how it seemed that I was naturally part of this family, even though I only understood half of what was said!

Lunch over, Mr Wortmann demonstrated for me his amazing photography equipment, showing how the huge zoom lens got every last bit of detail from even the tiniest of blooms. Such magnification needed more than a steady hand could deliver and a tripod and remote shutter cable was required. The rest of the family had seen all this before, and even though Heidi had held back for a moment, she soon joined the other women and they wandered slowly back in the direction of the hotel. Mr Wortmann was in his element, with someone new to show off to, but I wasn't able to give him my full attention and, whilst not wanting to appear rude, I kept glancing over my shoulder to see how far away the ladies had got. He explained that he had found a few rare plants that he hadn't catalogued yet and wanted to stay put and get that done properly. He sensed my impatience.

"But you vill vont to zee Heidi…of course. Please go on ahead," he said, beaming at me and gesturing towards the three women with his hand.

"Okay, Mr Wortmann," I agreed thankfully. "See you later."

He patted me encouragingly, almost affectionately, on the back, and I set off. I didn't want to run but wanted to join them as quickly as I could so I strode over the clumpy clifftop as speedily as I felt was safe. Luckily, the ladies were well aware of my dilemma and were idling along very slowly to give me the easiest of jobs to catch them up. I reached them within ten minutes. Heidi turned to see where I was and sent me the most wonderful smile as I got near.

"Papa iz impozible ven he zees a new plant," she apologised. "He must photo it, count zer petals and leaves and write it in his book. He can't help it!"

"But Paul is interested too," teased Mrs Wortmann, winking at me. "Aren't you, Paul?"

"Up to a point, yes," I conceded, "but learning about rare Dorset flora wasn't my main reason for being here today!" And without thinking, I put my hand affectionately on Heidi's shoulder and squeezed it. Heidi blushed and then raised her hand onto mine and squeezed it back. Mrs Wortmann smiled warmly and gave Julia an almost imperceptible nudge to get her walking ahead with her. Julia took the prompt, and they walked on together.

"I told you she likes you," Heidi whispered, coming close.

"She's very kind," I whispered back and turned her to face me and kissed her.

We walked hand in hand about fifty yards behind and then I surprised her.

"I can come over to Frankfurt and see you at the end of October."

Heidi looked at me amazed. "You vill come to Frankfurt for a day to zee me?"

"No, I will come to Frankfurt for five days to see you!" I replied beaming. "At the end of October. I will take time off work, use some holiday, *mein Urlaub*," I explained, making it as clear as I could.

She stopped dead in her tracks, staring at me with wide eyes, as if she couldn't quite believe what she had heard. She cocked her head on one side, frowned and repeated, as if for her own benefit and understanding. "You vill come to Frankfurt five days to zee me in your holiday at ze end October?"

"I can if you want me to," I confirmed.

Her face lit up with a huge smile, and she jumped into my arms. "I vont, I vont!" She laughed loudly.

We carried on our walk talking non-stop about what needed to be arranged. I could easily book a flight from Heathrow, but if she or her parents could find a small local hotel that wasn't too expensive and book it for me, that would be really helpful. I would pay for everything, of course. We reached 'The Lymes' at around two o'clock. I plucked up the courage and asked Mrs Wortmann.

"I would like to take Heidi and show her the hotel where I am staying if that's okay, please?"

Mrs Wortmann hesitated a moment and then smiled. "Okay, but back by zree, *ja*?" And she added, as if to make the deadline more important, "Kurt vill be back by zen."

"Yes, of course, thank you," I agreed.

Heidi and I quickly got into my mini, and I drove back to 'The Grafton'. It only took a short time before I had parked in the small hotel car park. Heidi laughed at the shabby exterior of the building.

"Not like ze Lymes!" she accurately observed.

"Not at all like 'The Lymes'," I agreed, shaking my head.

We went straight to reception. Gordon Grafton was stood behind the counter attending to a rather elderly guest who was clearly rather hard of hearing.

"Here's your key, Mrs Bentley," he shouted, pushing the key across the counter towards her. "Number seven as always, so you won't get lost!"

He shot a glance my way and raised his eyes to the ceiling theatrically. I smiled sympathetically back. The old lady made a shaky grab for the key and almost got it to her coat pocket but missed, and it fell to the floor. It seemed that she wasn't only hard of hearing but not very mobile either. She shuffled around in a kind of semi-circle using a stick to support her, anxiously looking down at the dark wooden floor for her key but not seeing it. Heidi sprang to her aid, nimbly scooping up the key and placing it into her hand, making sure that it was safely there, her hand remaining in Mrs Bentley's for a long moment. Mrs Bentley looked at Heidi with a smile of pure gratitude.

"Thank you, young lady," she said, "thank you very much."

Heidi smiled back and bobbed a semi-courtesy, bowing her head slightly forwards in acknowledgement of the status befitting an older generation. Mrs Bentley smiled back even wider and moved off in the direction of her room, pausing to pat Heidi affectionately on the shoulder as she passed.

"Bravo!" said Gordon appreciatively, looking at Heidi with joy and surprise. "Wonderful manners. Thank you."

Heidi blushed but smiled back.

"Room number two for Mr Gardener," announced Gordon grandly and got my key dramatically from the little key cupboard.

"This is my friend Heidi, Mr Grafton," I confirmed proudly, putting my arm around Heidi, then to her, semi-confidentially, "Mr Grafton owns the hotel." Of course, she already knew that, but I hoped it might spark something entertaining from him. He bowed slowly in her direction.

"Proprietor and general manager," he enlightened her, standing back up straight and looking important. "It may be a small hotel but keeping it going to my own high standards is a full-time occupation."

"I have a present that I want to give to Heidi, Mr Grafton," I said, being a bit formal on purpose. "I'll show her my room too and we'll be back down in half an hour so I can take her back to her family."

"Okay, Mr Gardener," he agreed, being equally formal. "Half an hour it is." And he tapped his wristwatch to make the point that he would be keeping an eye on the time. "Grafton Hotel standards can stretch to that for trustworthy guests."

I showed Heidi my tiny room; we squeezed past the wardrobe and sat on the single bed.

"Ver iz ze bazroom?" she asked, looking at each of the four walls for a door.

"It's along the corridor. I share it with several other guests," I explained.

She burst out laughing. "Very complicated." She giggled. "Vot if zer is already zumvon in ver ven you vont it?"

123

"I wait!" I laughed back and crossed my legs to emphasise the predicament.

"Oh Got!" she sympathised. "Best go at 'Zer Lymes' bevor you come back tonight!"

She became suddenly quiet and serious and pushed against me on the bed. I hugged her tightly, and we kissed passionately. She lay back on the bed, and I lay half on top of her, still kissing. She had her hands behind my head ruffling my hair and pulling me closer. Eventually, we needed a break.

"I have a gift for you."

She frowned, not understanding.

"A present," I explained, "you said you liked presents."

Heidi looked excited and sat up. "Oh yes," she agreed, "I love presents!"

"Well, I hope you like these," I said, getting the small bag out of my case. "It's not much but, well, they are from me to you."

She took the bag eagerly and carefully opened it, peeking inside. She pulled the record out first and took time to read the song title and artist from the label in the centre. She clearly knew the song and the lyrics and looked at me with wide, slightly watery eyes, knowing that I meant those words for her.

"It iz a beautiful zong," she said a bit emotionally and reached out a hand towards me.

"You are a very special lady to me," I confirmed back, taking her outstretched hand and kissing it.

She held my eyes for a long time and then went back to the bag. She took the little jewellery box out carefully, looked at me a bit anxiously and opened it. She seemed very happy and a bit relieved to see the silver St Christopher inside.

"So that you can wear it when you're back in Germany and have me close to you," I said and helped to put it on around her neck, taking care not to catch her hair in the little clasp that fastened the sliver chain.

"I vill alvays vear it," she said seriously, holding the little circular silver pendant between her fingers before tucking it beneath her t-shirt. "You are very kind." And she leant forward and kissed me gently.

I looked at my watch. "Time to go back to 'The Lymes'," I said sadly. "We should be back by three like your mother asked."

"*Ja!*" she agreed and got up from the bed carefully so as not to bump into the wardrobe.

I expected to find Gordon Grafton behind the reception counter checking his watch for our thirty-minute deadline, but he wasn't there so I left my key, and we drove back to 'The Lymes'.

I waited in the garden whilst Heidi went back to her room to put the record somewhere safe and then find her family. It took a lot longer than I had expected, but I enjoyed the afternoon sunshine and the happy buzz of the hotel, full as it was of many new guests. Alec appeared with a tray full of drinks for a nearby table. He waved cheerfully at me with his free hand and came over as soon as he got free.

"Well, well, Mr Gardener," he laughed, greeting me with outstretched hand. I shook it warmly. "Hi, Alec, thanks so much for getting my message to Heidi. We met up pretty much as intended."

"Excellent," he replied. "No problem at all. Where are you staying?"

"The Grafton Hotel," I confirmed in a grand tone for fun.

"How is Madame?" he asked, playfully pushing his lips out into a pout.

"Mr Grafton…Gordon, is great fun." I laughed. "We are getting on fine, just fine."

Alec nodded, smiling broadly. "He's harmless enough and quite entertaining I find," he agreed. "Are you with us for dinner tonight?"

"I really don't know, Alec," I said truthfully. "Heidi hasn't told me about any arrangements yet. She just went to find her family." And as I said it, I heard the unmistakable sound of loud German conversation as The Wortmanns entered the garden.

"Well, I guess you're about to find out!" Alec concluded, tipping his finger to his forehead in farewell and set off towards the bar inside for further refreshment orders.

Mr and Mrs Wortmann greeted me and laughed about the 'little zeatre' in which I was staying. Heidi had given them all of the details with some considerable exaggeration by the sound of it. I was invited to join them for dinner at seven o'clock and accepted with enthusiasm. We sat in the garden and drank tea, Mr and Mrs Wortmann were ever more curious to hear about my upbringing in Sunbury-on-Thames, what the schools were like, how the education system worked, more detail about what Dad did for a living, what my job entailed, what it was like working in London, how my studies were going and when they would finish, the price of houses, how I had started to play football, etc, etc. Julia was clearly getting very bored of this so, even though it was interesting for Heidi to hear, they went off together for a walk along the beach and then to play on the machines in reception. I was sure that Heidi believed that she could win another £50 jackpot!

I got on very well with Mr and Mrs Wortmann. We had a naturally flowing and enjoyable conversation. I never felt interrogated even though they were clearly making sure that I was the right kind of person for their daughter to be spending time with and, indeed, the right kind of person to allow to come and see her in Frankfurt. All went well and the girls came back at about six o'clock wanting showers and time to themselves before dinner. Mr and Mrs Wortmann wanted the same so I took myself off for a gentle walk along the beach and ended up in the bar having a drink and waiting for them to arrive. The bar was busy with new guests getting the feel of the place and making new friends, establishing relationships with Alec and the other bar staff that they hoped would stand them in good stead for their week ahead.

I took my beer to a small table in the corner and kept out of their way, happy to let them take centre-stage; their holiday week was ahead of them, after all.

I saw the Wortmanns arrive and seat themselves at their favourite table, got up and joined them. We had an excellent meal, great food, much laughter about the week we had enjoyed, plenty of wine for Mr and Mrs Wortmann which fuelled plenty of information about Frankfurt, where they lived, how they had met, a fairly precise account of their wedding day, which Heidi and Julia both really enjoyed as they hadn't heard it all before! Time passed really quickly, and as we finished our desserts, we realised that we were amongst the last in the restaurant. The bar was still busy though and rather rowdy! Plenty of action on the two machines in reception too. Alec will be pleased, I thought, after all his efforts to make sure that they were safely installed. Heidi and Julia wanted to play 'Dig-Dug' so I said goodnight to Mr and Mrs Wortmann and we left them waiting for coffee. We waited fifteen minutes for 'Dig-Dug' to become free and spent a happy hour watching Julia improve and progress to level seven. Both girls were tired by ten thirty and so was I. I said goodnight to Julia. Heidi came out with me to the car and we kissed, hugged and said goodnight. I drove slowly back to 'The Grafton', retrieved my key from Gordon and had an excellent sleep despite the small and uncomfortable bed.

Sunday – The Grafton Hotel

I woke up at seven thirty and went straight along the corridor to the bathroom to be sure that I got in first. I showered and shaved. After dressing, I went down to the restaurant/breakfast room. The tables were nicely set with chintzy tablecloths and vases of small summer blooms in the centre. Mrs Bentley was already seated and drinking tea. She waved at me cheerfully. I noticed that her hands were shaking badly and the cup rattled noisily in the saucer as she put it down.

"Good morning, Mrs Bentley," I shouted over. "Enjoy your breakfast." She nodded back, but I wasn't sure that she had really heard what I said.

Gordon Grafton minced into the room carrying a tray with a boiled egg and a rack of toast for Mrs Bentley. He smiled broadly at me as he went over to her table. He set it all down very carefully for her.

"Chef's best!" he shouted. "Enjoy!"

He came over to my table, drew his notepad dramatically from his waistcoat pocket, took his pen from behind his ear and raised his eyebrows expectantly at me.

"And what can we get for Paul on this bright and sunny morning? I may call you Paul, mayn't I?" he asked, smiling broadly again.

"Yes, of course," I agreed. "Chef's best boiled egg and toast for me too please, and do you have Earl Grey tea?"

"We certainly do," he confirmed as he scribbled my order firmly onto his pad. "Big plans for today?"

"Just time with Heidi," I said, wondering what we were actually going to do. "Time with her is always fantastic."

"Yes, I can imagine," he replied. "She is a very pretty girl with a nice way about her." He beamed, winked at me and minced off to the kitchen.

My tea arrived quickly followed soon by my egg and toast. The egg was perfectly cooked, lovely and hot with a delightful golden liquid yolk. The toast was good too. Not overdone or dry. I wondered how Mrs Bentley managed to get into her egg with her incredibly shaky hands. I guessed it must be practice!

I finished off my toast and drank the last of my tea. Gordon Grafton re-entered the room.

"That was really good, Gordon. Excellent," I said genuinely. "The best boiled egg and toast I've had in ages."

He came closer to my table, put his hand affectionately on my shoulder and inclined his head to one side, accepting the praise.

"Chef will be delighted to hear that," he replied, nodding his head. "Any more tea or toast?"

"No, thanks," I confirmed, "I'll get my stuff sorted and settle the bill in reception."

"No rush, no rush," said Gordon, and then, looking in the direction of Mrs Bentley's table, he said, "I have to clear that up first. What a mess!"

I decided that to try and defend her now would be futile and so went back to my room. I was packed and ready by nine thirty. I had said to Heidi that I would be at 'The Lymes' by ten o'clock.

I went down to reception and waited for Gordon. He bustled past grumpily towards the kitchen, a tablecloth and napkins bundled up in his arms.

"Be with you in a minute" – he grimaced – "I swear she eats that egg up through the tablecloth!" I laughed, I couldn't help it and thought that he must be fantastic on the stage.

He returned, gathering his composure and smoothing his colourful waistcoat as if removing unwanted crumbs. He got the big black book from under the counter, consulted the relevant entry and looked up at me smiling.

"Mr Gardener, one night only, bed and breakfast, £10.90, please. Was everything to your satisfaction?"

"Good, thank you, really good. I will be writing to the Swanage press to recommend The Grafton Hotel." And I gave him £12.00.

"Service is included in the £10.90," he corrected me.

"Just a small gesture of my appreciation," I said, smiling and extending my hand.

He took it in both of his and shook it firmly. "Always a pleasure to look after a gentleman!" He beamed. "Enjoy your time with Heidi today, Paul. The weather should be perfect."

I thanked him again, put my bag in the mini and drove the short distance to 'The Lymes', stopping to fill up for the return journey home on the way.

Heidi and the rest of the Wortmann family were already seated in the garden having had their breakfast. I joined them and shook hands with Mr and Mrs Wortmann. Heidi stayed in her seat beaming at me, telling me with her eyes that she didn't want to be too affectionate with the rest of her family there. I noticed that she was wearing her St Christopher.

"Ve vill go to Poole today. Zer iz a good park zer viz a lake," advised Mrs Wortmann. "Ve vill take a picnic."

"Sounds good," I said happily. "The weather is going to be perfect for a picnic."

Heidi looked a bit sulky.

"Ve vont to go on zer beach," moaned Julia.

"Zen go!" offered Mr Wortmann. "Ve vill vait."

Heidi and Julia looked at each other, laughed and got up to go and get their swimming gear on. Heidi gripped my shoulder affectionately as she passed. I didn't want to get my stuff from the car and get changed just for a quick dip in the sea so I stayed chatting with Mr and Mrs Wortmann. Heidi and Julia returned in their bikinis; I went down to the beach with them. We played catch, sat and chatted about what may be at the park that would be fun to do.

"If there's a lake, then there may be rowing boats for hire," I guessed. "Have you ever rowed a boat before, Heidi?"

"No," she answered, sounding interested. "Have you?"

"Oh yes, quite a few times," I replied. "It's not that difficult, and it isn't windy today."

"You can teach me!" she confirmed, clapping her hands in excitement.

"It's not that exciting." I laughed. "But it is fun. Will your mum and dad take one too? Sorry, no, your mum won't go near the water, will she?"

"No, she vownt." Heidi shook her head firmly. "But Papa will take Julia."

They went for a short swim, came back up the beach freezing cold and sat with their towels around themselves warming up in the sun. Eventually, Julia said, "Time to get ready." And she flicked her head up in the direction of the hotel garden. She got up and stumbled clumsily over the pebbles towards the steps. Heidi wasted no time, leant over and pulled my neck towards her, bringing my head to hers. We kissed deeply.

"Oh Got, Paul." She sighed. "Vy ve have to be viz zem all day?"

"We'll have some time in the rowing boat...if there is one," I said optimistically, gently pushing her hair away from her eyes. "At least, we can be together today rather than me be at home."

She smiled and turned to face me, nodded and got up to go but stumbled forward on a large, painful pebble and fell onto me. I half caught her and managed to save her from hitting any stones. My hands ended up half under her arm pits and half on her chest.

"Oops!" She giggled, looking suggestively down at where my hands were and shuffled back a fraction so that her breasts moved fully into my hands. I looked straight into her eyes, and she raised her eyebrows, intensifying her gaze. She moved her shoulders slightly side to side so that I could feel her firm breasts moving against my hands.

I took a deep breath and then whispered, "Wow, Heidi that's fantastic, but I think we should be careful who can see us."

She looked quickly around and saw that the beach was quite full of other guests. Luckily, none of them were looking at us. Heidi smiled and closed both eyes tightly, shimmied her shoulders back and forth again and then shuffled backwards, steadying herself with her hand on my shoulder and stood up slowly. I got up carefully too and followed her clumsily across the pebbles to the steps. She had taken one step up and I patted her backside affectionately, as if to hurry her along.

"Hey!" she objected half-heartedly, turned and wagged a finger at me playfully. We laughed and completed the ascent of the steps.

Mr and Mrs Wortmann had organised the picnic, and as soon as the girls were changed, we all got into the Mirafiori Estate and Mr Wortmann drove us to Poole park. It was a typical seaside park, quite large, with areas of trees providing welcome shade for picnicking, a children's play area with swings and slides and so on and a large boating lake. We walked slowly around the lake looking carefully at it. Mrs Wortmann looked a little anxious until we pointed out that the water was only four feet deep and lifejackets had to be worn in the boats. She relaxed and smiled at her husband.

"You vill take Julia zen?"

"And Paul vill row viz me!" Heidi jumped in. "I vont to learn how!"

Mr Wortmann pretended to object. "Oh no, Heidi, you vill zink ze ozer boats! Don't let her, Paul!" We all laughed and Heidi gave her dad a playful shove towards the water.

Julia, as always, was hungry, so we sat and had our picnic under some trees. Mr Wortmann tried to explain to Heidi how to row. How important it was to keep the oars in ze…"Vot are zey called, Paul?"

"Rowlocks," I confirmed.

Mrs Wortmann snorted out a loud laugh. "Careful of zer rollocks!" she spurted.

"*Row-locks!*" I said slowly, correcting her obvious mistake.

"Oh, row-locks," she repeated in a put-on, posh English accent.

We all laughed and congratulated her on her perfect pronunciation.

"The other thing that is very important," I carried on, "is that both oar heads are fully under the water before you pull back on them. Otherwise, you will fall backwards into the bottom of the boat and the oars may be lost!"

I demonstrated sat on the ground, mimicking 'catching-a-crab' and falling back, legs in the air. Much hilarity from all Wortmanns.

"Ve vill votch Heidi do zat!" Mr Wortmann laughed, and to his wife, he said, "Get a photo, *liebchen!*"

Half an hour later, picnics settled in our stomachs the four of us made our way down to the boathouse. There were already a few couples out on the lake.

"Watch that man, Heidi." I pointed to a man rowing very nicely. "See how he is rowing gently but strongly. No snatching or jerking of his oars."

Heidi pulled a serious face and mimicked the rowing action. Julia sniggered.

"But you vill teach me in ze boat!" Heidi insisted.

Mr Wortmann kindly paid for the two boats, and we awkwardly put on the uncomfortable lifejackets. Julia selected a red boat and Heidi picked a light blue one.

"You have an hour on the water," advised the boatman, "but I'm not that strict. If you want a little longer, that's okay. We're not busy yet."

We thanked him and he held the red boat alongside the pontoon whilst Mr Wortmann and Julia got in. Julia wobbled precariously for a moment but sat down safely in the back of the boat laughing. Mr Wortmann settled himself on the centre bench facing Julia. He secured the oars in the rowlocks and raised them whilst the boatman gave him a gentle shove to get going. Same again for me and Heidi in the light blue boat. We drifted away from the pontoon, and I started to change direction and row along the bank away from where Mr Wortmann was heading. I watched him slowly rowing along. He was leaning forward a bit too much but doing okay. I pulled on both oars to get the boat moving in a straight line now and with more speed.

"It really iz eazy!" Heidi observed from the back seat as we made progress away from her dad and Julia. She turned in her seat and waved to Julia. "Ven can I try?" she asked.

"Whenever you want," I replied, "but maybe watch me for another five minutes."

"Okay, boss!" she teased.

I showed her how to steer the boat right and left, keeping one oar raised out of the water, how to turn the oar heads into the water and then keep them straight, how to use her legs to power back on the oars and gain some speed. She was getting impatient!

"My go now!" she insisted.

"Okay," I agreed and pulled the oars into the boat. "You come over to the centre bench first." She moved slowly off the back seat, keeping low, her legs bent and then held onto me. I moved sideways on the bench to let her sit in the middle. Once she was safely there, I moved to the back seat.

"Bravo!" called out Heidi, mimicking Gordon Grafton from the day before. I smiled and clapped her excellent impersonation.

"Okay, now put the oars carefully back into the rowlocks one at a time," I encouraged.

Heidi twisted a little and found the oar on her right. She held it and pulled it up.

"Zis iz heavy!" she said grimacing.

"It's much lighter once it's in the rowlock," I replied. "Do you need help?"

"No!" she came back quickly, clearly she was going to do this herself!

Having got the right oar in, she did the same with the left.

"Well done," I encouraged again.

The oar heads were floating on top of the water as Heidi leant her weight onto the handles.

"Now make sure that the oar heads are just under the water and are vertical." I held up my hand like a karate chop with my fingers held close together. Heidi checked each oar head, adjusted one and then nodded. "Ready," she confirmed.

"Now push your hands and arms forward together like I did and pull back using your legs to push through the stroke. Pull your tummy muscles in at the same time," I helped.

She slowly followed the instructions, and we moved forward. "As you finish the stroke, push the oars up a bit so the heads are out of the water as you bring them back," I directed. Heidi did exactly that, and we carried on forwards.

"I can't zee ver I'm going," worried Heidi.

"Don't worry, I can," I replied. "It's all okay, just keep going straight; you're doing really well."

Inevitably, one of her arms was stronger than the other so the boat headed slightly towards the bank. That was corrected with an extra stroke or two with her left oar and she carried on well again.

Heidi was delighted with herself.

"I can do zis!" she shouted. "Let's go farzter." And she pulled harder on the oars.

"You're really good at this," I congratulated her, "we're nearly at the far end of the lake."

Heidi needed a little help to negotiate the turn and then decided it was my turn to row again. We carefully swapped places, and Heidi looked for her dad and Julia. They were at the other end of the lake, and it looked as though Julia was having a go.

"Vot do you really vont to do in your life?" asked Heidi earnestly, looking straight at me.

"Wow, what a question!" I replied, thinking hard. I left it a long time before answering. "I want to be happy and that means being with someone who loves me. Everything else follows on from that." I waited for her response.

"You zay zomeone who loves you," she replied, thinking out loud. "Don't you need to love zem too?"

"Yes, of course," I agreed, "but I said it that way because I would not be happy being with someone that I loved but who didn't love me. You're right, it has to be both ways." I waited again to see if there was any further reaction. There wasn't, so I changed the subject. "How's Julia doing?"

Heidi had a long look past my shoulder. "I zink she lost one!" She giggled.

"Oh dear, maybe we should help," I suggested and started to row more quickly towards them. When we got close, Julia was in fits of giggles and shouted something in German to Heidi.

"Zlow down, Paul," she said. "It iz just here, but zey can't reach it."

I slowed the boat right down and Heidi scrambled over to the side. The whole boat tipped over alarmingly with her weight, but she stayed calm and reached down into the water and pulled up Julia's lost oar to much cheering and applause from her father, who had taken back his position on the centre bench. Julia was in the back of the boat in uncontrollable giggles.

"She let go!" complained Mr Wortmann. "She just let it go!"

Heidi was in fits of giggles too by now, endangering our dry state by rocking the boat from one side to the other.

"Let's go back in now whilst we can, Mr Wortmann!" I shouted. He agreed, and we both rowed carefully back to the pontoon.

"It's okay, you have another ten minutes," called out the boat man.

"We're quitting whilst we're still dry!" I laughed.

Safely back on dry land, we re-joined Mrs Wortmann who had been reading a magazine in the sunshine.

"Gut fun?" she asked.

"*Ja, ja!*" Julia laughed. "I lost ze oar!"

"Oh, problem viz ze rollocks?" she asked, emphasising the mispronunciation of the word.

"Alvays!" spluttered Heidi.

It was half past three now and I wanted to be away by four to miss the worst of the traffic so Mr Wortmann drove us back to 'The Lymes' and the family assembled in the car park to say goodbye until the end of October. I shook their hands and gave Julia a hug. Heidi and I went to the end of the garden near the bike shed to be alone. We stood very close.

"I vill miss you," she said quietly, "very much. I vill write often."

I took her in my arms and hugged her tightly and then kissed her gently on the lips, on the nose and on the forehead.

"I'll miss you too. I'll think of you every day," I said emotionally. "I'll write back straight away and tell you all my news. Take care of yourself, Heidi." I stroked the back of her head and put my forehead gently against hers. We stayed like that for a few moments and then I stepped back.

"I have to go," I said and looked one last time into those beautiful blue eyes. They were welling up so I kissed her again, turned and walked back to the car park. Heidi stayed where she was a moment and then ran across and waved frantically at me as I drove out of the car park.

Part 2
September 1978
Frankfurt, Germany

The Boy Fun Flirt Club

It was the first meeting of the Boy Fun Flirt Club since the summer holidays. An important meeting. Ute Stroebel waited patiently in her room for the others to arrive. There were only three members of the BFFC, herself included. All three of them gorgeous, 17-year-olds, studying for their higher exams at the same school in Frankfurt. It was Ute's club, her creation. She had handpicked the other two, Sylvia Kranz and Heidi Wortmann. She had known them a long time; she could trust them. Well, she knew things about them that gave her the power to have certainty of their trustworthiness. She had made sure that each of them privately knew of her knowledge of their separate secrets. No one else knew of the club nor its purpose. Ute had founded it over twelve months before, straight after her humiliation by Werner Hartwig, bastard. She had made the stupid mistake of falling for him, following him around like a little lost dog, waiting for him to turn up for dates, waiting and waiting all on her own, knowing deep down that he wasn't coming but waiting nevertheless, too devastated to give up and go home. He had played her along for weeks when finally he had written a large note and posted it on the college common room noticeboard, officially informing her that he was no longer her boyfriend, that he didn't want her following him around anymore, it was over. When she had gone into the common room on that June afternoon, there was a crowd of girls around the noticeboard laughing and reading it out in mock male voices. They went suddenly silent when they saw her, moved away quickly, embarrassed but waiting to enjoy the next few minutes. She had approached the board suspiciously, slowly and gradually took in the title of the note. It was for her, her name underlined in thick black pen. The rest became a bit of a blur. She read and re-read the note, tore it off the board and stormed home with it. Once home, she re-read the note and cried. Loud sobs of anger and upset that she vowed would never happen again. In fact, the opposite. Her sworn purpose became the entrapment and humiliation of as many stupid boys as possible, but it would be more effective with some help. Hence, the Boy Fun Flirt Club. Sylvia and Heidi certainly helped to widen the options, execute the plans she created, shared in her celebration of victories, contributed to the growing 'shrine' of photos, love letters and gifts that Ute so carefully looked after and displayed at each meeting to remind them all of what could be achieved.

It was Sunday, 10th of September. The meeting should start at ten. Sylvia would be on time, but Heidi would be late, always! She would blame the tram, or her watch was slow or this or that. It didn't matter; she would be there too. She had done quite well so far. She had a kind of playful innocence that a certain kind of boy found irresistible.

The doorbell rang and Ute beat her mother to the door and let Sylvia in. She had a bag with her, promising. Her mother called to her, checking everything was all right. Her poor, lonely, divorced mother, who now struggled on her own to do the very best she could under the circumstances.

"All okay, Mum. It's Sylvia," she called back in the direction of the sitting room.

Sylvia was ushered into Ute's bedroom. The BFFC poster was proudly mounted on the wall behind the bed. They had all contributed to the design, the fervent declaration and the colour scheme. Ute had coffee and biscuits ready in her room, and they both partook without waiting for Heidi. They chatted for a while deliberately avoiding the business topics that could only be discussed once all three were present.

"Come on, Heidi!" moaned Ute. "Where is that girl?"

"She's always late, Ute," Sylvia said evenly, smoothing the situation. "She'll be here, don't you worry."

They drank their coffee, ate biscuits and waited, now in silence. At ten past ten, the doorbell rang. Ute sprang up and answered the door. Heidi stood looking hot, flustered and apologetic at the same time.

"Sorry, sorry. The first tram was full so I had to wait for the next one, and it's such a long walk from the stop to your flat," she garbled.

Ute said nothing and stood looking at her, taking in her good deep summer tan, brown against her yellow, blonde curly hair, making her wait now in the corridor of the apartment block. She smiled and welcomed her in shooing her through the entrance hall into her bedroom.

They all embraced, as was the ritual of the club. No silly shaking hands here, they were sisters with a mission. Heidi was given a coffee and biscuit, and they all sat down on large cushions on the floor.

Ute noticed approvingly that Heidi also had a large bag with her.

"Now, ladies, the Boy Fun Flirt Club is in session!" Ute announced happily. "How were your summer holidays?" She looked enquiringly at Sylvia.

"My week in Portugal was good," she said. "Mainly German boys where I was though, no handsome locals really. I have a couple of phone numbers and some photos to show."

"Anything worth developing?" asked Ute, probing for more detail.

"Mostly, they were the usual beach kind who don't want to get too involved, you know fun on holiday then home, but there was one geeky kind of guy that I worked on."

"Tell us more," encouraged Ute.

"Dietrich Franke," continued Sylvia. "He's a bit pale and skinny and likes cartoon books. He brought some with him on holiday and showed them to me. Quite expensive American ones I think. He goes to an import shop in Hamburg to buy them."

"Is that where he lives?" asked Ute.

"Yes, he's from the North!" Sylvia laughed. Ute giggled; Heidi followed.

"He gave me two that I pretended to like and said he would get in touch to let me know how he's getting along. He's studying sciences at college. He wants to be an industrial chemist, whatever that is. Anyway, here he is!"

Sylvia took a small photo album from her bag. She flicked through the album. "Here is the hotel where we stayed, here is the beach and bars and here is Dietrich." She handed the album over to Ute.

"Oh my, he is pale and skinny!" She laughed. Heidi strained over her shoulder to see. "Well, let's wait for his first letter and then we can all create a reply from you. Maybe he can be persuaded to visit us from Hamburg in the North! Who knows what fun we might have if he can be enticed by his beautiful Sylvia? Did he say he liked you?"

"He didn't say much like that, he's very shy, but he did try to kiss me on our last day there."

"And?" pushed Ute.

"I couldn't bring myself to do it," replied Sylvia quietly, waiting for the rebuke. "My mum and dad were watching."

"Oh, Sylvia!" protested Ute. "You know what we're here for! It's not to enjoy a boy's kiss or touch but to trap him. One kiss for Dietrich could have secured some excellent letters, gifts and maybe even a visit. You must be ready to go further to get results."

"I know, I'm sorry, but I do have the cartoon books." She dug in her bag and pulled them out. "For our collection," she offered hopefully.

"Okay, well done for that," conceded Ute taking them and putting them on her bed. "Well, I had a fairly boring summer here in Frankfurt," went on Ute. "Mum couldn't afford for us to go away with what my father left her, bastard. I walked into the city several times on the lookout for likely tourists. I always wore my short skirt and no bra for maximum effect and had some photos taken with some cheesy Americans but nothing worth following up I think." She produced her own photo album and showed the other two some bright images of her, looking very sexy surrounded by excited, overactive American boys in front of the Rathaus, the main station and on one of the bridges over the Main. "They were all too busy with their stupid tourist schedules to even stop and buy me a drink," she complained. "I got tired of doing it in the end…and my feet hurt in those high heels!"

"Cheapskates, you look gorgeous in that outfit," said Sylvia, "I don't know how they resisted."

"Most were with their parents and had no say in what they could do," replied Ute. "Anyway, I pretty much drew a blank this time. How about you, Heidi?"

"England was great, thank you," Heidi started. "Three weeks seemed a long time in the same place, but my dad had his special research to do, you know plants and insects and so on. The first week was a bit boring. The weather wasn't great and there were no boys of the right age in the hotel…but in the second week, Paul arrived."

"Oh, Paul, okay," cooed Ute. "Tell us more, Heidi. This sounds promising."

"Well, Paul came with his sister and parents for the second week. He's nineteen, has his own car, a good job in London and is good-looking and funny." Heidi continued, "He came after me straight away. He speaks German too."

"Wow, well done," chimed in Sylvia. "What's he like?"

Heidi got out her photo album and handed it over to Ute. She carefully opened it and took time with each photo. "Nice English hotel," she observed, "and right by the sea too. Nice garden and views and…oh, here he is…red hair too, a ginger-nut!"

"I like his red hair," objected Heidi.

She got a stern glare from Ute. "Heidi! Heidi Wortmann, we are not supposed to be attracted, just attractive." Her voice softened. "But he does have a good body, look, Sylvia." And she handed the album over to an eager Sylvia.

"Okay, yes," she mused, trying not to sound too positive, "and a bit of a show-off here too." She pointed to a photo of him spinning a ball on his finger on the beach.

"Yes, he's good at basketball and football," advised Heidi.

"So what happened?" asked Ute directly.

"Well, on his first day, I bumped into him accidentally in the restaurant. Then he and his sister got me and Julia to join in a ball game on the beach, then we went to a lake and a castle."

"Who went?" asked Sylvia.

"Me and Julia and his sister, in his car. He has a dark green mini. That was the second or third day I think."

"And then?" encouraged Ute.

"I got scared in a thunderstorm and he held my hand. Also, we all went to a pub and played skittles."

"What are skittles?" Sylvia asked, looking baffled.

"A bit like ten-pin bowling but old fashioned," explained Heidi. "Our team won!"

"There must be something that you did just with him?" questioned Ute.

"Yes, he took me for a bike ride. It was hard to get my parents to agree, but I managed."

"Good girl," congratulated Ute. "So what happened?"

"Well, it was hot and we got tired and laid down in a field for a rest. He told me that he liked me a lot and kissed me. It was a nice kiss so I kissed him back, just quickly on the lips." Heidi paused and looked at them both, expecting more questions or some reaction.

"Okay, more please!" urged Ute.

"On a rainy day, he took us to see *JAWS 2*, but Julia got scared. He was kind to her, and we left early. Then we played a new video game machine. 'Dig-Dug' they call it. That was fun, and I won a £50 jackpot on a fruit machine!"

"But what about this Paul?" persisted Ute.

"On his last evening, we played cards and needed a pen and paper to write down the scores so I went with him to his room to get them, and he kissed me properly. A really good long mouth-to-mouth kiss. It lasted ages."

"Did you like that?" asked Sylvia.

"Oh yes," Heidi assured them. "We did it a lot after that!"

"I thought you said it was his last evening?" queried Ute. "How could you kiss him a lot if he went home?"

"He came back the next weekend," explained Heidi.

"Oh wow!" exclaimed Sylvia. "You really hooked him Heidi!"

"He stayed in a nearby hotel with a funny gay hotel owner," she continued, "and he gave me these." Heidi took a small bag from within her larger one and took out a record. She handed it to Ute who studied it carefully then passed it on to Sylvia.

"*Three Times a Lady*," Ute whistled in appreciation, "dedicated to our gorgeous Heidi by a ginger Englishman."

Heidi hesitated, her hand still inside the small bag. She knew that Ute had noticed and took out the small dark blue jewellery box.

"Oh my God," blurted out Sylvia, "some jewels too!"

Heidi opened the box and handed it to Ute. She took out the delicate silver chain and pendant and held them up in front of her face, draped over her fingers.

"So he can be close to me when we are apart," Heidi said quietly.

Ute looked triumphant. "Well, these go to the very top of our collection," she said as she put them onto her bed. "I am super proud of you, Heidi. What a great job you have done. I'm sure that you swapped addresses and that we will soon receive the first of many wonderful love letters from your Paul. We will be able to write sincere, loving sentences and get his replies in both English and German on a regular basis until we decide to drop him from a great height!"

"He's coming here at the end of October," said Heidi, almost to herself.

"What! What did you say?" Ute pounced on the revelation. "He's coming here, to Frankfurt to see you?"

"Yes," Heidi confirmed, "at the end of October. He has a week holiday from his work."

"Oh my God," Sylvia blurted out, "I never thought...I mean...he met you for a few days on holiday and is paying to fly to Frankfurt to see you again? Did you have sex with him, Heidi?"

"No, I did not." Heidi looked furiously at Sylvia. "He's coming because he wants to. I did not ask him to."

"Well, we must make him most welcome!" purred Ute pensively. "Where will he stay?"

Heidi calmed down. "My dad will book a small local hotel for him, not too expensive, convenient for where we live. They like him, my parents."

"Oh, really?" quizzed Ute. "I hope that won't complicate things."

"What do you mean?" enquired Heidi.

"Well, we can't have your parents messing up any plans that we have for him when he's here!" Ute replied firmly.

"They will expect to see him, to spend some time with him, Dad will be home with us because it is half-term week," Heidi reminded them.

"Yes, of course, not a problem," Ute replied calmly. "As long as we know when he will be free to be with you…I mean free for the plans we will create together." She had a thought. "If it's the end of October and half term, then it will be Silvesterball practice week! What an opportunity! Does he waltz, Heidi? I bet not. We can arrange for him to sit at a table whilst you dance closely with your partner, Gerd, isn't it? We can make him sit on his own and watch all evening long whilst we all dance, you with your Gerd, when he cannot. He can stew there getting more and more jealous! Perfect. Oh, there is much work to be done, girls, and not much time."

"Do you know the exact date he will be coming yet, Heidi?" followed on Sylvia. "We must arrange to meet him at the airport!"

"With your new boyfriend!" added in Ute, clapping at her spontaneous idea. "Yes, with your new German man. Who could that be? Maybe my cousin Michael will be able to help there. He's the right kind of age. He will surely help me."

Heidi had enjoyed the previous BFFC cruel 'games' that they had played on boys none of them liked, but she was feeling a bit apprehensive about this already.

"We must write a letter to your Paul straight away, right now, to make sure that he doesn't change his plans," directed Ute and got up to fetch pen and paper and sit at her desk.

"My darling, Paul," she started, "I am back home in Frankfurt now and cannot think of anything but you. The days go by so slowly when I think of our time together in…Where was it, Heidi?"

"Swanage," confirmed Heidi.

"Swanage," Ute repeated, writing it down.

"I remember our first kiss on that bike ride," chipped in Sylvia. "In the warm sunshine. It is crazy, but I love you."

"Yes, yes!" encouraged Ute. "Keep going!" And she wrote it all down.

The letter progressed through the morning and into the afternoon. Ute also noted down other ideas to be developed for the visit, to fill the available days of that week with outings and situations designed specifically to humiliate and hurt this boy. His love for Heidi would be torn apart by the end of the week, his heart broken, ready to return home with nothing.

Thursday, 26th October

Frankfurt, Germany

The plan was set, and Ute wanted to run through it one last time with the BFFC girls. Heidi and Sylvia were with her in her bedroom. They had read Paul's latest letter to Heidi. He was fully committed to his flight from Heathrow the following morning. He could hardly wait to see her again.

"Here we go then, girls," said Ute, in charge as usual. "Let's run through the plan one last time. I have double checked with all of the others and all are absolutely ready to play their part. Day 1, Meet Paul at Frankfurt airport at three o'clock. Heidi will be with her new boyfriend (Michael). They will be arm in arm when he arrives through the 'gate'. Heidi will wave in a friendly way so he can see her but stay arm in arm with Michael. No one will go forward to help with his case or bags. He will manage on his own. Heidi will smile nicely and shake his hand (NO KISSING!) and introduce him to all of us.

"We say 'Hi' but then stay talking to each other, not to him at all. We all go to the tram station and get the tram with him to Waldschmidt Strasse and the Hotel Splendid. Heidi will sit next to Michael and pay him special attention, not looking at Paul at all, not once. The rest of us will sit in twos, or stand if there is no room, but no one will sit or stand with Paul. He must be on his own with his bags – none of us close by to talk to. We all get out and show him his hotel. Heidi then shakes his hand, says goodbye and see you tomorrow at nine thirty in the hotel reception. We all walk away, Heidi with her arm around Michael, and get onto the first tram we can wherever it is going. Paul will have the Wortmann family telephone number and may ring it to see what is happening. All that needs to be said is that Heidi will meet him in his hotel reception at nine thirty in the morning and tell him the plan for the week. All clear?"

Heidi and Sylvia nodded, Sylvia smiling and looking excited.

Ute continued, "Day 2, Heidi meets him and takes him back to the Wortmann family flat for a day out with them all. No Michael that day but Heidi will explain how she met him and how he swept her off her feet. Sorry for the bad timing but that's life! The day runs as if he is a relative, not a 'lover boy' from your holiday. No touching, holding hands or getting too close. He is like your cousin, Heidi, one you have to put up with when he is sent over to visit."

The conversation went on in great detail, day by day. Ute careful to direct each activity emphasising the precise interaction with Paul, especially at the party that she had organised at Michael's parents' house and the night out in the old town at the disco…they would find out if he could dance at all.

Then the centrepiece event at the Silvesterball practice at the Frankfurt Zoo ballroom.

"If he gets so upset that he catches the next flight home before the end of the week, then we will have succeeded even better than we expected!" concluded Ute and closed the meeting.

Friday, 27th October

Heathrow Airport, England

"Come on, Paul," called Mum, "I want to get you to the airport in good time to get your flight."

I had packed for the week, checked I had everything I needed, double checked for tickets, Deutsche Marks, credit card, passport, English-German dictionary and phrase book, phone numbers for both the Wortmanns' apartment and the 'Hotel Splendid' where I was staying. Heidi had written and confirmed that her dad had made the booking. It was all confirmed. They would meet me at Frankfurt airport at around three o'clock. My flight was scheduled to land at two thirty German time so that should give me enough time to collect my suitcase and get through passport and customs checks. I was used to travelling by plane so Heathrow held no fears for me. I knew the layout and the procedure for each stage well enough. British Airways staff were always very helpful if needed.

"Coming, Mum," I shouted back, "nearly ready."

It was nine o'clock. Heathrow was only thirty minutes' drive from home. I would have masses of time to check my suitcase and myself in and get to the departure gate before the eleven o'clock deadline.

I was excited. Heidi's last letter had been especially wonderful. She'd remembered every last detail of the special times together in Swanage and seemed to have planned so much for my visit. It was so lucky that it was half term week for her and I could be with her virtually all of the time. Everything was carefully placed on the back seat of the car. Mum beamed at me as we sat in the front, she knew how much this meant to me.

The drive to the airport was easy, no traffic hold ups. I kissed Mum goodbye at the drop-off point and promised to phone her from the hotel when I got there. I went into the airport with my suitcase. Flight BA0726 to Frankfurt was already on the electronic departure board with 'ON TIME' in the middle column. Take off scheduled at 12.00. It was too early to go to the departure gate, and it wasn't allocated yet anyway so I found a café and had a coffee. I sat reading Heidi's first ever letter to me. I kept it in the inside pocket of my jacket. I re-read the precious words that had leapt from the page at me the first time I read them, "*Es ist Verruckt, aber Ich liebe dich.*" It is crazy, but I love you.

She loved me, really loved me. She had written it down so that I should have no doubt. I had written straight back confirming my love for her too. We had exchanged seven letters in the nine weeks since we had last seen each other in

Swanage. Heidi's were full of news about what was going on at college, preparation for the Silvesterball dance practice and plenty of wonderful romantic messages. There were photos enclosed too. Some of us together in Swanage, Wortmann family ones and two of her good-looking college friends, Ute and Sylvia. She said I would probably meet them at some time during the five days.

I killed time by wandering around the luxury duty-free shops but had no intention of buying anything. All my spare money had been spent on the flight and the five nights at 'Hotel Splendid'. I had held back just about enough for whatever we did in those five days.

Finally, the gate number showed on the electronic board, and I made my way casually over to it. I showed my boarding pass and passport and then sat and waited. I listened carefully to the German conversations going on but couldn't understand a lot of what was said. Most were business people in business suits talking business language.

A middle-aged lady came and sat next to me. She looked a bit nervous and sat with her hands clasped in her lap. From what she was wearing and from her facial appearance, she looked English.

"It's good that the flight is on time," I said in a friendly way, "saves any last-minute panics!"

"Oh yes," she replied, seeming grateful not to have to sit in silence, "I haven't flown on my own before. I was always with…" – her sentence trailed off – "with Bill," she finished quietly.

I realised quickly that this conversation could get emotional if I wasn't careful so I decided not to ask anything about Bill.

"I'm Paul," I said, smiling and extending my hand for a shake. "I've never been to Frankfurt before, but I am used to flying so please don't worry. If you need any help, just ask me."

She shook my hand warmly. "Oh, thank you," she replied, looking relieved. "I'm Evelyn. I'm going to see my son; he works in Frankfurt."

"Well, it's not a long flight and everything will be very straightforward. Are you going for a long visit? Did you check a suitcase in?" I asked.

"Yes," confirmed Evelyn, "I checked my suitcase in. It's a red one, makes it easy to see it on the conveyor belt! I'm in Frankfurt for a week."

"I have a suitcase to collect too," I advised, "I'll make sure that I help you find yours at the other end."

"We can go through passport control and customs together too if you like?"

"You're very kind, that would be wonderful," said Evelyn, visibly relaxing back into her seat and un-knotting her hands. We chatted a bit. She had come from Guildford by train and then taxi. She didn't drive. Her son, Greg, was meeting her at Frankfurt airport. I told her about Heidi, our holiday in Swanage and the plan for the week.

"How romantic," she said enthusiastically, "lucky you."

I showed her a photo of Heidi.

"Oh, she's lovely," said Evelyn. "She looks full of fun too."

We were called to board the plane on time and the flight was uneventful. I looked around for Evelyn after we had landed at Frankfurt. She was looking for me too and remained sat in her seat until she could see me.

"Here we are, Evelyn, safe and sound," I said as she came forward up the aisle. "We'll get our cases and be through to the arrivals gate in no time!"

She smiled gratefully, and we walked together carefully following signs for 'Baggage Reclaim'. "Do you speak German?" asked Evelyn.

"Enough to get by but certainly not fluently. They always have the signs in English as well as German," I replied, pointing at one to prove the point.

We quickly found Evelyn's red case and waited for my grey one. Evelyn stood patiently waiting with me rather than going on alone.

Cases safely in hand, we joined the short queue for passport inspection and then walked slowly through the green 'NOTHING TO DECLARE' customs section. I had briefed her whilst we waited for our cases that it is always best to walk through slowly and to keep talking in a relaxed, natural way so that the customs officers are not suspicious. We glided through without any attention from the German customs men.

"Phew," said Evelyn once we were out the other side. "That always makes me so nervous, especially when they have those big revolvers strapped to their belts."

"The 'keep talking' trick always works!" I grinned.

Evelyn gave me a hug, thanked me for all my help and went off in search of Greg.

I walked through the arrivals gate with several others and looked for the Wortmann family. I didn't see them. There were a few groups of teenagers laughing and chatting but no Wortmann family. Then, wait a minute, was that Heidi with that group? It looked like her from the back, but she was in the arms of some tall, dark-haired bloke. It couldn't be her. I stopped, put my case down and looked again. Then I recognised the faces of Heidi's friends, Ute and Sylvia from the photos she had sent me. Maybe it was Heidi. One of the group nudged her, and she turned around, her left arm still around this bloke's waist. She smiled and waved. It *was* Heidi. I walked slowly forward, feeling confused, unsure and a little sick. She stayed where she was, chatting and as I reached her, she held out her hand.

"Hi, Paul," she said cheerfully. "Good flight?"

On autopilot, my head buzzing, I shook her hand.

"Er, yes, all on time," I replied looking straight into those bright blue eyes, mine puzzled and worried.

"Good. Ve'll take you to your hotel on ze tram," Heidi confirmed.

The whole group moved quickly off as one, almost military fashion. I picked up my case and followed, having to hurry to keep up. Heidi was still arm-in-arm with this bloke at the front of the group, leading quickly.

Was this a joke? Some kind of test? Was I supposed to stop and shout 'Wait a minute! This is all wrong! Stop messing about!'

If it was a joke, then they weren't ready to give it up yet. I hurried along behind them, down some stairs, saw the 'Tram' sign and followed down an escalator into a dark, dimly lit tunnel then eventually out the other end into the light and onto the street. There were several other queues of people boarding different trams. Heidi and the group waited by Tram Stop 7. I joined them. They carried on their German conversations. No one turning to speak to me. Then a tram arrived. They got on and one of them turned and said, "Follow us, ve vill pay, just get on viz your case."

Obediently, I followed. The tram was full, but I managed to stow my case near the door and stayed with it for fear of losing it in the crowd. The group had mingled in with the other travellers, and I couldn't see Heidi. What was going on? I felt the inside pocket of my jacket. The letter was still there. The letter in which Heidi had clearly written that she loved me. This *was* a joke! We would all get off the tram and she would laugh, punch my arm and hug and kiss me. I smiled to myself. Cheeky cow! I'd get her back later in the week. I'd think of something!

Three stops later, Ute and Sylvia pushed past me to get to the door and pressed the red button. A bell rang and the tram slowed to a stop and Ute said, "Zis iz ver ve get out."

The group piled out of the opening tram doors. I lumbered slowly out with my case and saw a road sign 'Waldscmidtstrasse'. I slowly walked over to the group, in my mind allowing them time to enjoy that last bit of the joke and waited for Heidi to come over to me. She didn't. She stayed at the head of the group, arm-in-arm with this bloke and called back over her shoulder.

"Ze hotel iz just here – *links*." And she waved her hand towards a building ahead and walked on. I followed…okay, a few minutes more of the joke then a proper 'Hello' at the hotel. Five minutes' walk up Waldschmidtstrasse, there was a grey three-storey concrete building with a 'Hotel Splendid' sign halfway up the outside wall. It looked anything but 'splendid'! In fact, it looked quite foreboding. The group stopped outside, taking up most of the narrow pavement. Heidi said, "Here it iz, your hotel." She leaned against this bloke, her arm around his waist. I put my suitcase down and stepped straight towards her. Just for a second, I detected

161

fright in her eyes, but it disappeared and she smiled, her eyes bright blue and gleaming but not with any warmth, not with love.

"Ve vill come tomorrow morning after breakfast at nine zirty. Ve have a family day out in ze forest. *Tschuss*." And she waved, turned and the group walked off up the street.

I stood and waited for them to stop and turn and laugh and come back and for Heidi to fling her arms around me. I stood and watched them go. When I was certain that they weren't turning around, that this was real, there was no joke, I picked up my case, went into the 'Hotel Splendid' reception. I checked in using my best German and went up to Room 39.

I put my suitcase on the floor by the neat little single bed and sat down at the tidy little desk with my head in my hands. I didn't dare look into the mirror in front of me. It felt like I had been punched very hard in the stomach. I was short of breath, my head span. I was stamping my feet involuntarily on the floor in frustration and anxiety. I couldn't concentrate on anything.

I had promised to phone Mum and tell her that I had arrived safely and looked around for a phone. It was there by the side of the bed. I went over and picked it up to check for a dial tone. It was live. I put the receiver down and looked at the floor.

What was I going to tell her? I was here but what had gone wrong? What the hell had just happened? What would happen tomorrow? For the rest of the week? This was not the Heidi Wortmann I had fallen in love with in Swanage.

The End